KU-080-053

THE
WILFUL PRINCESS
& THE
PIEBALD PRINCE

BY ROBIN HOBB

THE FARSEER TRILOGY
Assassin's Apprentice
Royal Assassin
Assassin's Quest

THE LIVESHIP TRADERS
Ship of Magic
The Mad Ship
Ship of Destiny

THE TAWNY MAN
Fool's Errand
The Golden Fool
Fool's Fate

THE SOLDIER SON
Shaman's Crossing
Forest Mage
Renegade's Magic

THE RAIN WILD CHRONICLES
The Dragon Keeper
Dragon Haven
City of Dragons
Blood of Dragons

The Inheritance

WRITING AS MEGAN LINDHOLM
The Reindeer People
Wolf's Brother

Harpy's Flight
The Windsingers
The Limbreth Gate
Luck of the Wheels

Cloven Hooves
Alien Earth

ROBIN HOBB

THE
WILFUL PRINCESS
& THE
PIEBALD PRINCE

SOUTH DUBLIN COUNTY LIBRARIES	
SD900000114473	
Bertrams	01/11/2013
	£14.99
	TA

HARPER
Voyager

HarperCollins*Publishers*
77–85 Fulham Palace Road,
Hammersmith, London W6 8JB

www.harpercollins.co.uk

Published by Harper*Voyager*
An imprint of HarperCollins*Publishers* 2013
1

Copyright © Robin Hobb 2013
Illustrations © Jackie Morris 2013

Robin Hobb asserts the moral right to
be identified as the author of this work

A catalogue record for this book
is available from the British Library

ISBN: 978 0 00 749813 0

This novel is entirely a work of fiction.
The names, characters and incidents portrayed in it are
the work of the author's imagination. Any resemblance to
actual persons, living or dead, events or localities is
entirely coincidental.

Printed and bound in Great Britain by
Clays Ltd, St Ives plc

All rights reserved. No part of this publication may be
reproduced, stored in a retrieval system, or transmitted,
in any form or by any means, electronic, mechanical,
photocopying, recording or otherwise, without the prior
permission of the publishers.

MIX
Paper from
responsible sources
FSC www.fsc.org **FSC˙ C007454**

FSC is a non-profit international organisation established
to promote the responsible management of the world's forests.
Products carrying the FSC label are independently certified
to assure consumers that they come from forests that are managed
to meet the social, economic and ecological needs
of present and future generations.

Find out more about HarperCollins and the environment at
www.harpercollins.co.uk/green

Part One
The Wilful Princess

At Redbird's request do I, Felicity, write these words. He was a lettered man and could have undertaken this venture himself had fate allotted him time for it, but it did not. He earnestly put this task upon me, entreating that I be nothing but truthful, as befits the memory of a truth-speaking minstrel, and that I write in my clearest hand, for he wished that these words be plain to any who might read them, next year or a score of years hence. He charged me, too, to write of things only I can know so that in years to come no one can say that what they read here was but a minstrel's fancy, a fillip added to history to make it a juicier tale.

So I will write these words twice, as he did his song, and bind them together in two packets. One I will place in a hidden place known only to me, and the other I will hide where Redbird said it will likely remain well hidden for years: the scroll library at Buckkeep. And so the truth may

be hidden for days or weeks or even decades, but eventually it will come out!

Much of this tale is Redbird's tale, but I will preface it with a story that not even he knows in full. For it is only when his tale and mine are told side by side that the full significance of them can be understood.

Now Redbird was a minstrel and a truthsinger, one sworn to his king to sing only the true songs, the histories and the records of the realms. Not for him tales of dragons and pecksies and maidens enchanted to sleep for a hundred years. No, his task was to observe, and remember, and tell plain only and exactly what he saw. And so I shall honour his profession and his ways, for truth and truth only shall I trap here in my letters. And if it be a truth that ill pleases folk these days, at least it will remain somewhere for someone to find some day and know the true blood of the Farseer lineage.

My part of the tale begins when I was a little girl. My mother and I were both there on the name-sealing day for Princess Caution Farseer. Queen Capable was radiant in an elegant gown of green and white that set off her dark eyes and hair. King Virile was dressed in well-tailored Buck blue, as was fitting. And the little princess was naked, as custom decreed.

Princess Caution was six weeks old at the time, a well-formed child with a crop of curly dark hair. My mother, her wet-nurse, stood by with a heavily embroidered coverlet and a soft blanket to receive the child after the ceremony. I stood at her side, better dressed than I'd ever been in my life, holding several clean white flannels in the event of any accidents.

I didn't listen to the words of the sealing ceremony. At three years old, I was too intent on what I had heard was going to happen to the baby. She would be passed through fire, immersed in water, and buried in earth to seal her name to her and be sure that she would express the virtues of it. So, as the flames in the brazier leaped high and the queen held out her little daughter, I caught my breath in terror and anticipation.

But the queen barely waved the child through the smoke. One flame might have licked at her rosy little heel, but the princess made no murmur of objection. I did. "But she didn't go through the fire!"

My mother set her hand on my shoulder. "Hush, Felicity," she said gently, and backed the admonition with a sharp pinch.

I clenched my lips and kept silent. Even at three, I well knew that a pinch was a warning of worse things to come if I disobeyed. I saw that the child was barely submersed in the water before the queen snatched her out of it, and that scarcely a trowelful of dry soil was dribbled down her back, never touching her head and brow at all. The little princess was startled but not weeping as the queen handed her over to her royal father. Virile lifted her high, and the nobility of the Six Duchies solemnly bowed before the Farseer heir. As her father lowered her, Caution began to wail, and Virile quickly handed her to her mother. Even more swiftly, the queen passed her to my mother. Wiped clean and wrapped in her blankets, Caution settled again, and my mother returned her to the queen.

I remember little more of that day, save for a comment I heard passed from one duke to another. "She was under the water so briefly the bubbles didn't even rise from her skin. Her name was not sealed to her."

The other shook her head. "Mark me well, Bearns. Her parents will not have the heart to raise her as sternly as they ought."

On the day that Princess Caution Farseer was born, my mother had weaned me. She should have weaned me when I was two, but when she learned that Queen Capable was with child she kept me at the breast to be sure that she would still be in milk when the royal infant was born. My grandmother had been Queen Capable's wet-nurse, and had won the promise from her mother that when the time came her own daughter would likewise serve her family. It was our great good luck that Lady Capable grew up to wed King Virile. Queen Capable might have forgotten her mother's promise, but my grandmother and mother certainly did not. The women of our family have long had a tradition of providing for their daughters as best they may. We are not a wealthy family nor of noble lineage, but many a high-born child has been nourished on our rich milk.

I lived at Buckkeep with my mother during the years she suckled Princess Caution. My mother saw to it that from the first day the princess was entrusted to her care, I served her royal highness. At first, my duties were small and simple: to fetch a warm washcloth, to bring a clean napkin, to carry a basket of soiled little garments down to the washerwomen. But as I grew I became the princess's servant more than my mother's helper. I held her hands for her first toddling steps, interpreted her babyish lisping for adults too stupid to understand her, and helped her in all ways that an older sister might help a younger one. If she wanted a toy, I fetched it for her. If she finished her bread and milk and wanted more, I gave her mine. For my mother whispered into my ear every night before I slept, "Serve her in all things, for if she makes you hers, then you have made her yours as well. Then, perhaps, as you grow, your life will be easier than mine has been."

So, from a very early age, I gave way to the princess in all things. I soothed her hurts, quieted her tantrums, and indulged her in every small way that I could. It was me she wanted to cut her meat, and me who tied her slippers. My bed was beside my mother's, in the room adjacent to the

Princess Caution's nursery. When she had a restless night, an evil dream or a teething fever, I often slept in her big soft bed beside her and she took comfort from my presence. I became invisible, as much a part of the princess as her little green cloak or her lacy white nightdress.

Queen Capable was a doting but not attentive mother. She adored the sweet, calm moments with her baby, but quickly surrendered the child to my mother's care the moment Caution became soiled, fractious or trying. That suited my mother well. She always did her best to give the queen exactly the experience of her child that she wished to have. I marked well how this benefited my mother and me and in my childish way I mimicked this behavior with the little princess.

Caution was not sickly, but neither was she a hearty infant: even when she could hold her own spoon she was fussy about what she ate. The only food that she never refused was the milk of my mother's breast. Perhaps that was why she was allowed to nurse long past the age at which most children are weaned, but the more likely reason was that the little princess was never refused anything she wanted. She had only to shed a single tear and all past rules were overturned that she might be the exception. She was over four years old when finally she gave up the teat, and only because my mother caught summer fever and her milk dried up.

Nobler women than we had long been waiting a chance to tend the little princess and win her regard. As soon as it was known that my mother's milk was gone and Caution weaned, a better-born nanny was brought in to take my mother's place, and nobler playmates offered to her.

When I returned with my mother to our cottage and the stony fields my father tended, all seemed strange to me. I had grown up at Buckkeep and had only the vaguest memories of my own home. I had seen my father and elder brother at intervals, but did not know either of them in a familiar, comfortable way. They were too busy with the chores of our farm to have much time for me. My mother turned her efforts to getting with child again, for only then would her milk return and another wet-nurse position be offered to her. It was her career and what she expected to do for as long as she could bear a child or give milk to someone else's.

I was not glad to be there. Our house was small and our living conditions rude and rustic after the comforts of Buckkeep. No rug shielded me from the rough floor; no tapestry blocked the wind that crept through the plank walls of the loft where I slept. Food was simple and my portion smaller than when I had been the princess's table mate, setting her an example of how to eat well and heartily. Nonetheless, when on the third day after our return a messenger arrived to fetch me back to Buckkeep, I was not pleased to go. I heard with satisfaction that Princess Caution missed me, that she wanted nothing to do with other playmates, that she would not sleep at night but had cried and fussed ever since I had left. The princess had demanded that I be returned to her, and the queen herself had sent the messenger to fetch me back. But I had been at my mother's side for nearly every day since I had been born, and I did not wish to be separated from her.

I was not quite seven and I dared to yowl when my mother announced that I would be glad to go. We left the messenger staring while my mother dragged me up to the loft to pack my clothes, and brush and braid my hair. It was there that she gave me the sharp slap that quietened me. As I sobbed and she folded my clothes and tucked them into a bag, she gave me the most succinct advice surely that ever a mother gave a small daughter. "You are crying when you should be rejoicing. This is your chance, Felicity, and possibly the only one I can ever give you. Stay with me, and you will have to marry young, bear often, and nurse children until your breasts sag flat and your back never ceases aching. But go with the messenger now, and you have the chance to become the princess's confidante and playmate, despite our low birth. Make much of her at all times, always take her side, intervene and intercede for her. You are a clever girl. Learn everything she is taught. Make first claim on her cast-offs. Be indispensable. Perform every humble task for her that others disdain. Do all these things, my little one, and who knows what you can make for yourself and of yourself? Now, dry your tears. I hope you will remember and heed my words long after you've forgotten all else about me. I will come to see you as soon as I can. But until then remember that I loved you enough to put you on this path. Give me a hug and a kiss, for I will surely miss you, my clever one."

Slapped, counselled and kissed farewell, I followed her down the ladder from the loft. The messenger had brought a pony for me to ride back to Buckkeep. That was my first experience astride a horse, and the beginning of my life-long distrust of the creatures.

By the next day, I was back at Buckkeep, reinstalled in the small servant's chamber off the princess's own bed-room, and back into Princess Caution's daily routine. That night, the queen herself sat at the foot of her daughter's bed while I stood beside her and sang lullaby after lul-laby until Princess Caution drowsed off. For that service, I received a queenly smile, a pat on the head and a scowl from the royal nursemaid who had been displaced from the chamber next to the princess' own. It was the first time I found myself squarely at odds with my fellow servants, but it was not to be the last.

I never lived in my father's house again, but my parents did not forget me. Every few years, my mother came to court as a wet-nurse, for she had found favour with the noble ladies for her calm and competent ways. We often found ways to see each another. She guided me in how I managed the princess and gave me much wise advice. Whenever I thanked her she would say, "There will come a time when I cannot nurse a baby any more, and then life will be harder for me. I hope that when my fortune turns, you will remember that I gave you up to put you on a better path than mine." And always I would promise that I would.

"The baby princess grew, as all children grow, and became beautiful, as some children do, and developed a stubborn will of her own such as most parents most heartily wish no child of theirs ever does." So the minstrels have sung of her, but it is not fair to think she spoiled herself. Caution was a princess, and her mother was a queen. And Caution was the only green and growing sprig on the royal tree, and so she was indulged. Despite being Caution's favourite companion, I was deemed too young to care for her alone. The nursemaid bore the brunt of Caution's wilfulness. Flung dishes and shrieking tantrums were daily events. The nursemaid strove to take a firm line with the princess, but the moment the royal heir was banished to scream and kick alone, I was at her side, to soothe and comfort her. Did I know then that I was encouraging her wilfulness? Not on a reasoning level, but I recognized that

I could be to her what no one else was. I can only defend myself by saying that I regarded the princess as mine in a way that she belonged to no one else. I resented it when others sought to discipline her or force her into any action. I loved her: she was my baby, my sibling and my future. So I suppose that in some ways I was partially responsible for her headstrong ways.

At first, it was only in small things that Caution demanded her way. She would wear her yellow skirts every single day, not her green ones or her red ones or even her blue ones with the white ruffles all round. Her yellow ones only would she wear, even if they were muddied and needed mending. Nor would she accept a different set of yellow skirts, no – not even if the fabric had been woven by the same weaver and the hems stitched by the same seamstress. Only her first yellow skirts would she wear. So the laundress and the seamstress toiled by night so that the yellow skirts were presentable every morning. I trotted willingly down the stairs every night to the washing court bearing the yellow skirts, and no one had to wake me at dawn to again make that journey to bring my princess the freshly washed and pressed skirts. I saw to it that it was always from me that she received them. Whenever I could, I took credit for any good thing that came to her.

As she got older and her presence was required more often in formal settings, it was I who fastened her slippers and fluffed her skirts and smoothed her jet-black hair before she went out the door. And when, as often happened, the occasion ended in a royal tantrum by the overtired child, I was the one they sent for, to coax and pet her back into a cooperative frame of mind and get her to bed.

As she grew, Princess Caution demanded her way in larger things. From refusing any skirts but her yellow ones, she went to demanding a cascade of stylish and elaborate garments. She would not eat the meat of cattle nor swine nor fowl, but only on venison would she dine, morning, noon and night, winter or summer. And so the huntsman must hunt and the butcher must dress his kills all year round to make sure her meals pleased her, even when the season was not right for the taking of a deer. Her father,

taking a stand with her at last, declared that perhaps his daughter would be more reasonable if she saw the extent of the work that her habits required. Thus, she was less than ten when he took her on her first hunt. It troubled me, for I did not like horses and did not ride with pleasure. But Princess Caution insisted I must accompany her and, as I always did, I gave way to her.

If her father had thought to dissuade Caution, that hunt was the wrong tack to take. She rode well, as she had from

the first time she was set on a horse, and kept up easily with the lead riders. She saw the stag brought to bay, saw the dogs bring him down and be whipped off him, and took no discouragement from any of the wild and bloody scene. I was spared that sight for I had lagged far behind the pack and only caught up with the party as they were preparing to return home. But I might as well have been there, because for days afterwards the princess talked of little else.

In one regard the king succeeded, for his daughter became a huntress in her own right, and expanded her diet to include any game that she herself brought down. So she provided pheasant and duck for the table, venison in plenty and even wild boar as she grew stronger and more capable. Only when hunting did she abandon my company, but as it put her often at her father's side and among his nobles, the king rejoiced in his offspring's new-found interest. So I took care not to interfere, even if it did put her outside my influence. Instead, I became the willing listener for every exploit she cared to share with me. Indeed, I think that my own clumsiness on horseback and squeamishness at the blood delighted her. For so long I had been her elder and always the better at whatever we did. When I saw how pleased she was to have bested me, I took care never to compete with her, but always expressed my wonder at all she could do.

I realized then that she was growing up. As the difference in our stations became more and more clear to her, I took care not to overstep my place. And so, although I attended her lessons with her, and cut her pens and mixed her ink, I was careful that she never discovered that I could both read and cipher as well as she could. I took care to study at night, borrowing her scrolls while she slept, ensuring they were always back on her desk as if they had never been touched before dawn. It was the same when she received her lessons in history and later, in diplomacy and deportment. By then she was a young woman, wearing a simple tiara to show her rank. I sat on a low stool at her feet as the minstrels who sang the histories performed for her. I listened to her father's ministers as they lectured her on the dangers of Chalced and the intricacies of striking advantageous trade agreements with Bingtown. I learned what she did, and applied it, not to foreign powers, but to the shifting tides of influence within the court. I never forgot my common birth and lack of standing, but that does not mean I did not find ways to circumvent these obstacles.

As the court began to surround my princess with ambitious young noblewomen and eligible young lords, I learned to navigate my way through them. Given my plain face, evading the interest of the young males was easier than weathering the vicious storms of young female politics. Some of her companions resented me and took every opportunity to humiliate me. Others saw me as a path to her favour and courted me with kind words and small gifts. I would be hard-pressed to say which were the more dangerous. By day, I took care to be correct and unobtrusive. But in the evenings, when I was brushing out the princess's hair or folding her clothing to put away for the night, I told her any gossip I had heard, and spoke of which young woman I'd seen exchanging a token with a young man who was already pledged to another, and giggled with her over which girl was cursed with garlicky breath and which young man suffered from warts on his hands. I was her confidante, ever attentive and never critical of her. And if one in her circle had treated me with less than kindness, perhaps Caution heard more about that person's unkind comments about her hair, or dress, or skin. And if the princess became a bit cooler toward them, well, it was no more than they deserved.

At seventeen, grown to woman, the princess received the crown of the Queen-in-Waiting, as has always been our tradition in the Six Duchies. From now until the death of her father bestowed the throne on her, her royal training to rule would be in earnest. She would sit in the judgment chamber when nobles sought arbitration from the monarchy, to learn and eventually to share in the decisions they passed down. She would deal with diplomats and ambassadors from foreign countries, and travel within her own realm so that her dukes and duchesses should come to know and respect her. And suitable mates would be paraded before her. So, at least, was the purpose of that position.

Queen-in-Waiting Caution was not, perhaps, as dedicated as an heir should be but, as she confided to me, both her parents were in excellent health and had run the kingdom well for many years. Why interfere now, and spend decades in anxious waiting for an event she hoped was many years away? Now was her time to be young and to enjoy her life in a way that she never could once she was queen. Soon enough, she would have to bow her head to the heavy weight of a crown.

Soon her nobles muttered that at a time when she should have been learning the tasks of a ruler, Queen-in-Waiting Caution was instead learning only to indulge herself. Many a suitor was paraded before her, and many a noble son she spurned. By day and in public she gave polite excuses, saying she was too young as yet or that she wished to know herself better before she chose a mate for life. But in the evenings, as I brushed out her hair, she spoke her mind bluntly to me. That one was too fair, and the next one too dark. The Farrow lad giggled like a girl when he laughed and the one from Tilth brayed like a donkey. That one was too thin; nights with him would be like sleeping in the kindling pile. Another was too fleshy; she would be smothered in his embrace.

"What, then, do you want in a man?" I dared to ask her. A thin shard of green jealousy stabbed my heart but I took care not to show it. I was unlikely to marry well and when I did, my duties to my husband would likely take me from Caution's side. Once wed, my future would narrow to a swelling belly and a future as a wet-nurse, forever pregnant or tending children not my own. A husband I would have to find, eventually. But my heart did not cry out for a man. I drew the tortoiseshell comb slowly through Queen-in-Waiting Caution's sleek black hair, savoring the soft threading of it through my hands. I had all I needed there at my fingertips, for I loved her with all my being.

She had been pondering my words. Now she smiled. "Away, away with all of them! I shall choose my own man when the time is right, and only to please myself, for what else truly will matter? I will be queen, Felicity! Queen! I will know all I need to rule, and the decisions will be mine. What is the use of being queen if I cannot even choose my own mate? For now, while I have you, I need no man to share my bed." And she laughed as she turned to smile at me, and I smiled in return.

From my mother, I had learned that although all noble ladies must be virgins when they first wed, it did not mean they must be strangers to pleasure. And in that duty I had served my queen well and willingly since before we had been women.

But my question had set her mind on a different track of thought. She cocked her head at the mirror and a single furrow divided her brow. "And I am not at all sure that I will ever wish to share my throne or the powers that go with it."

"But what of getting an heir to the Farseer throne?" I dared to ask her.

"When the time for one is needed, I am sure there will be plenty of candidates," she said carelessly.

I wondered that she could care so little about it. It was true that she had cousins, and that they were well aware of the line of inheritance should Caution never bear a child. I knew that eventually her duchies would demand that Queen-in-Waiting Caution take a husband and produce an heir. Yet for now I was secretly well pleased that she felt no need of a man in her bed. I, too, felt that our current arrangement was pleasant enough.

Her eighteenth birthday came and went, and then her nineteenth, and she showed no sign of choosing a mate. All the while she was most wilful, not only in her own ways, but in encouraging the young women of her court to live as they chose regardless of what their fathers or mothers might say.

And, as the minstrels have sung, "Still the king and queen replied, 'Yes, sweet Queen-in-Waiting Caution. So it shall be.' For it seemed they could deny her nothing."

I shall not deny the truth of that song, but I will say that there was far more to Queen-In-Waiting Caution than the tales tell.

As her twentieth birthday approached, her nobles became more restless. Yet neither King Virile nor Queen Capable would listen to those who suggested Queen-in-Waiting Caution might be better off wedded and bedded. The Duke of Bearns, who had offered a son, said, "A woman bears easiest when she is young and strong of back."

The Duchess of Farrow, who had offered a nephew said, "Quench her woman's passions in a bed before she comes to the throne. She will rule better so."

The Duke and Duchess of Tilth, who had offered her a choice of their twin sons suggested, "The throne teeters on just a single heir. Let her wed young and mother many, to be sure the line is strong."

The Duchess of Shoaks, who had six daughters of her own waiting to wed, declared, "Let the princess choose a man soon so that others will know the berth is taken and be free to court other fair and noble maidens."

Only the Duke and Duchess of Buck were silent in these things. For the Duke of Buck was the king's own younger brother, Strategy Farseer, and he had been bound well and tight to his name. He looked down on his little son Canny growing strong and straight and made no murmur that Queen-in-Waiting Caution had neither wed nor produced an heir to the throne. If the crown should happen to fall upon his own son's head, I knew he would not mind the bump.

These things I saw and knew. More than once, I tried to speak of them to Caution. But even though I was as well schooled as she was, she dismissed my thoughts as the gossiping of her servant rather than the warning of a friend. A friend, I might add, who had been as close to her for many years as if I were her sibling, and loved her more truly than any of the ladies who fawned upon her. She dismissed my advice that she should soon choose for herself, or all choices might be taken from her. And that brought pain to me, for I had believed she thought more highly of me than that.

But wilful she was. And still I loved her.

It was not just in men that the Queen-in-Waiting would listen only to herself, but also in horseflesh. It happened in Buckkeep one summer, in that time when all bring horses and cattle to trade and breed, that a Chalcedean trader came likewise with his wares. On a ship he brought them, for at that time Shoaks was so wroth with the Duke of Chalced that the Duke would not suffer any Chalcedean folk to cross his lands. This trader was a sly fellow, far too thin for an honest man, with a patch on one eye, and a wet way of talking so that he hissed like a spitting snake when he spoke. All turned a wary eye on him and little he sold that first day. So I noticed, for I was there, sent by Queen-in-Waiting Caution herself to look over the Cattle and Horse Fair that year and bring back news of anything worth seeing.

Now among his wares this odd trader had a spotted horse – not dappled nor speckled, mind you, but blotted in great ugly spots, like a fruit that has taken blight, or a poorly dyed blanket, or a milk cow. Black-and-white he was, with a rolling blue eye on one side of his head and a dark staring one on the other. Big was this beast, and a stud, unruly of temper, screaming out his challenges to any stallion that came near and snuffing and stamping after every passing mare. He was a nuisance and a danger, and twice the guards had to be called to quell the beast. They warned the Chalcedean that he had best keep his horse to rights, or he would be thrown out of the fair. But each time, when the guards arrived, they found the Spotted Stud standing docile as a lamb, and at his head, holding his halter, a youth of strange mien.

He was not garbed well, but rather as a servant and a ragged one at that. He was silent in his ways, his eyes always cast down, and he spoke few words, fair or ill, to the guards for when he did speak he stuttered so that it

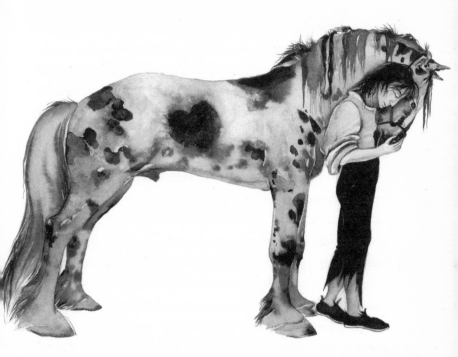

took him three times as long to say whatever he had in
his mind as it should have. Only to the horse he spoke
frequently, in a breath so soft none could make out the
words, but always the rumbustious horse turned docile as
an old mare at his utterances. Things are said of him now
that none know if they are true or not: that he never in his
days ate meat, but oft was seen standing beside his horse,
chewing a stem of grass. Some say the nails of his hands
were as thick and yellow as a horse's hooves. Others that

his laugh was a whinny and that when he was angered he pawed at the earth and stamped. I can say with absolute certainty that many of the things now said of him are rankest nonsense, and only spoken aloud to justify all that came afterward.

So when I went back to my mistress, I admit I spoke of the Chalcedean trader, and of the spotted horse and the man who tended it. But not, I swear, in a way to turn her head with thoughts of either one.

On the third day of the trading fair, Queen-in-Waiting Caution announced that she wanted to stroll the picket lines and see what the traders had to offer. Often, I fear, did Queen-in-Waiting Caution indulge herself in such strolls around the market on a trade day, when some folk felt it would have been more fitting to her rank sitting in her chair by her father's judgment throne, learning how to serve justice to her people. Such duties never amused Queen-in-Waiting Caution: she was often heard to say that when she had to ride a throne all day would be soon enough to take up that duty.

And so she and a circle of her more adventurous ladies had gone down to the stock markets. I was there, trailing after them, ready to carry any parcel or dash off to fetch a cool drink for her. I did not much enjoy the Cattle and Horse Fair. It was a hot day and dusty, and often folk passed us leading oxen or horses. I found it alarming when such large beasts passed directly behind or in front of me, yet the Queen-In-Waiting made nothing of that, but looked about with eager eyes, as did her ladies.

Yet it did not seem they were in a mood to buy, for with tart tongues and mouths full of laughter they made mock of first one trader and his wares and then another. This one looked as like to his horse as to his mother. That one's stud was more round-bellied than the pregnant mare he showed. This horse had a coat so rough it would sand a man's buttocks to his bones, and that one had a head more like cow. Such were the jests her ladies threw, and the Queen-in-Waiting did not rebuke their unseemly behavior, but laughed loudly in a way that only encouraged them to speak even more coarsely.

At last they came to the Chalcedean trader and his blotchy horse. The beast was peaceful that day, for the tight-lipped man who tended it stood at its head. When Caution and her ladies drew near, he looked up at her and his eyes were as full of wonder as if he had never seen a woman before. Despite his poor clothes, he was a handsome man, well muscled, tall and raven-haired. When the Queen-in-Waiting glanced at him, he blushed like a maid, and sank to one knee before her, bowing his head, and his thick black hair fell like a mane, cloaking him from her gaze. The fall of his hair bared the nape of his neck, and it was pale and downy as an infant's.

"Stop," said Caution to her ladies. "There is something here I wish to look at."

One of the ladies, thinking to prove her wit, pointed at the stud and said, "Oh, so that's what became of that blanket with the holes burned in it; they've used it to make a horse."

Another, vying for favour, said, "No, not at all. 'Tis but a spotted cow with a horse's halter on his head."

A third said, "Behold, not a cow nor a blanket, but a white cheese gone to black mould."

All laughed far louder than such jests merited, expecting to win Queen-in-Waiting Caution's laughter as well. But instead she spoke in a terrible voice, harsh and cold. "Silence, you fools! Never before have I beheld a creature as perfect as this one."

But when she spoke, her eyes were not on the stallion, nor on his Chalcedean owner, but instead on the young man who gripped the Spotted Stud's halter. There and on that spot, she declared that she would buy the beast. When the deal was closed and the gold passed, she had bought not just the Spotted Stud, but the man who held his halter, and this despite the laws of the Six Duchies against the buying or selling of a man. Slave he had been to the Chalcedean, but she in that moment raised him to free man and servant.

His name was Lostler. Now some will say that his name was Sly, and some will even call him Sly o' the Wit when they sing of him. I never heard him called by such a name. The flaw of his mouth made him prone to soft speech and shy ways; yet for all that he was a man, as hard-muscled and strong-willed as his horse. Soon all would come to know that as well.

Before the month was out, the Stablemaster of Buckkeep stood before the Queen-in-Waiting, begging her to be rid of the spotted horse. The stud would not tolerate anyone to handle him, save Lostler. The other stallions in their stalls screamed and snorted at his presence and could not be calmed, save by Lostler. The Spotted Stud leaped a fence and serviced three mares that were to have been bred to another – nor would he leave them until Lostler came to fetch him away. "Be rid of one stallion, for the good of your entire stable," the stablemaster told her.

To all this the Queen-in-Waiting listened and then she said, "It is not one stallion we need to be rid of, but one stablemaster. By your own words, Lostler does your work for you. Be gone, then, and let Lostler master my stable and horses for me."

So it came to be, for even in this matter her father the king did not oppose her, but let go the man he had himself raised to stablemaster a decade before and allowed Queen-in-Waiting Caution to put her own servant in his place.

Now let the truth be told. Lostler was a man with what some folk thought a gift in those days. He could whisper in the tongues of beasts, and so bend nearly any animal to his will. Some call this magic the Wit, and some speak of such a man as having the Old Blood, the blood that beasts and men once shared. It was no shame, in those days – not for one to have the Wit nor for one to use it. Some folk said then that much good could come of that magic. Certainly, in the year that followed, it is true that both horses and dogs in the stables prospered and many a sickly beast was cured and many a vicious animal made gentle. Many and many a spotted foal was born, for the blood of the Spotted Stud proved strong when mingled with the Buckkeep stock.

Whenever the Queen-in Waiting wished to ride out, Lostler prepared her horse for her, and held her stirrup for her to mount, and softly answered all questions she brought to him regarding her horse. She began to ride daily, even though in times past she had been indifferent to riding as a pastime, and only enthused for the hunt. Now, however, she began to find time each day for riding, and I, perforce, had to accompany her, regardless of how little I enjoyed it.

So it was that I saw how she was with her new stablemaster. Shy he was, this Lostler, flushing pink whenever she addressed him. But she spoke to him soft and gentle, in the very way in which he spoke to the horses. So also he listened to her, standing still, eyes downcast. Some said that she charmed him with her quiet words even as he charmed a hesitant horse.

Soon she declared she would ride the Spotted Stud, although all knew the beast's temperament was uneven and sometimes savage. "Only Lostler can manage him when he is in a temper," her nobles said to her, beseeching her to be more considerate. "If you ride such a beast for pleasure, few other riders shall take pleasure in accompanying you." To which she replied, "Then Lostler shall ride out at my side whenever I ride my Spotted Stud. He shall be there, to help me manage him if he becomes difficult. As for others, they may come along or not as they will, for I'm sure it will not matter to me."

So it transpired, despite what other folk thought of that and much to the king's displeasure. I, however, was never excused from such expeditions. Lostler chose a horse for me, one so gentle and spiritless as to be the equivalent of a cushioned chair. On that creature, my panniers laden with the morning repast, I trailed daily after the Queen-in-Waiting and her stablemaster. Most often we left the keep at a spirited gallop, something I did not enjoy and an exercise at which they quickly outpaced me and my decrepit mount. Yet before long, I would catch up with them and find them letting their horses plod sedately along while Lostler rode at Caution's side in quiet conversation with her.

Only I observed them: I knew what others only guessed at. When Caution stroked the muzzle of her Spotted Stud, or traced her fingers down his neck, Lostler was the one who shivered with pleasure. When she mounted the horse and rode him, it was as if she embraced the man. Beast and man were alike under her spell, and I began to see in my lady a sensuality that I had only suspected in all our years together. It was all the more painful to me that she lavished on this Lostler all her attention and charms while I became ever more unseen and forgotten.

So the days passed, and with each passing day, she paid more heed to her riding pleasure than to her throne. Still, noble youths came to seek her companionship for court-ship, but as often as not, to find time to speak with her they must try to court her while she rode her Spotted Stud and the stablemaster shadowed them, mute and mournful. Never did I stop loving my lady, and yet I will admit that I saw her take a sort of delight in how this tormented the shy man who followed her as she flirted with these suitors. And privately I thought the attention she paid any of these young nobles was not for the man himself, but only for how it pricked the heart of the stablemaster.

Came a day in the following autumn when the mists cloaked the morning and all the court rode out to the hunt. The Queen-in-Waiting said she would ride her Spotted Stud. So it was, but on that day, the king's will had prevailed in another matter, and Stablemaster Lostler was commanded to remain behind at the stables. There was a young man the king favoured who was to ride in the hunt, and the king made it most plain to his wilful daughter, in a conversation not intended for my ears, that he expected her to pay attention to this young man and his courting. This vexed Caution and she did not fail to show her irritation, being short of speech with those around her and riding her horse most aggressively. Very soon the hounds took up a scent, and streamed forth and all the horses and nobles followed them. The Queen-in-Waiting, on her capricious mount, was at the very front of the riders, and soon she surged ahead of all. As they rode, the mists of the vales rose thick, and the baying of the hounds echoed from the hills until one could scarce say from which direction the dogs gave cry. In the trailing shrouds of mist, Queen-in-Waiting Caution on her Spotted Stud were lost from sight.

Now some will say that the air smelled of magic that morning, and that soon the hounds were confounded and ran whimpering back to their handlers. Some will say that the mist swirled only about the Queen-in-Waiting and her mount, or that the Spotted Stud deliberately bore her into the thickest bank of fog, to conceal her as he carried her away from her nobles. But I was there and it was only a miserably wet and foggy day. My poor mount and I were jostled right and left and soon left behind in the hue and cry. I had expected it to be so, and as soon as the hullaba-loo of the hunt had gone, I was happy to turn my horse's head around and let him find his way back to the stables.

Hours later, when the hunters and hounds and handlers, dripping with damp and dispirited, returned to Buckkeep, the Queen-in-Waiting was not among them. Her noble suitor would not apologize for her being missing, saying plainly that she had sought to out-ride him, and she had. Then the king was wroth with all, and ordered up his men to go search for Caution. But before they could depart, all saw the Stablemaster Lostler ride out. Now, I have heard some minstrels say that he stood in the stable yard and proclaimed, "I will find her most swiftly, for where the Spotted Stud is, there too am I, and even in the mist our hearts call to one another." Thus it is claimed that with his own tongue he admitted his Beast-magic, though in those days there was small shame and little danger in owning to it. But I was there and he spoke no such words. He never called attention to himself or his stuttering tongue, so never would he have made such a public announcement.

And I will speak bluntly of the gossip that was noised about later and is still repeated even now. Some insist that the Queen-in-Waiting was never lost at all, but rode ahead of the pack and into a hidden vale, because she and the stablemaster had decided she should do so long before the hunt. Some will say when the stablemaster rode up to her, the mists parted to reveal her sitting on the Spotted Stud. I have heard one minstrel sing of how the mist cloaked her hair as with a thousand jewels, and tell of how pink her cheeks were with the chill. He sang, too, that she wept with joy to be found, and that when Lostler dismounted, she slid down from her own horse and into his waiting arms.

Oh, a hundred ways have their secrets been gossiped about and yet what really happened remains their secret to this day. Did Caution deliberately lose herself in some foggy vale, knowing that Lostler would come to seek her? Did Lostler whisper to the Spotted Stud to bear her astray and keep her hidden until he could come to claim her as his own? Some will say that he whispered to Queen-in-Waiting Caution as he did to the horses and dogs in the stable, and so bespelled her with his voice that she scarcely knew what she did. Some will say that he took her roughly, with no regard for her high birth, as a stallion will take any mare he pleases. Others will say, no, she could not wait to lift her skirts and pull him down upon her. Many say that it was her first time to do so, but by no means her last.

Since I was closer to her than any other and even I do not know the truth of any of it with certainty, I know that all the gossip and whispers are mere speculation, some of it more out of jealousy and hatefulness than any concern for the truth.

But this much is known, and truly. As the sun was leaving the sky, home they came, and there was mud upon Caution's skirts and twigs in her hair. She said she had taken a fall from her horse and needed some time to recover even after Lostler found her, and then that they had needed more time to discover their way home in the fog and gathering dusk.

I quietly noticed that she did not limp from her fall, despite the mud upon her skirts. And that she was in as fair a temper as ever I had seen her, humming in her bath and going to bed early and sleeping deep and well.

From that day forth, all noticed a change in the Queen-in-Waiting. There was a glow to her cheeks, and she took to riding out very early in the morning with only the stablemaster in attendance upon her and me trailing along behind. The wrath of the king over this was as nothing to her. As always, they began their ride with a spirited gallop, at a pace my horse could not hope to sustain. But in those days, I did not catch up with them as easily as I once had. Often I did not see them again until they came riding back to find me. Then Queen-in-Waiting Caution would be pink-cheeked and laughing at my worries and saying they must put me on a fleeter mount the next day.

But they never did.

There was a morning when they had outpaced me deliberately, marooning me behind them on my placid

mount while they rode out of my sight. I had no chance
of finding where they had gone, nor could I return to the
castle without inviting questions as to where my lady was.
The day grew hot as I plodded along and, seeking relief
from the sun, I turned from the trail and rode to the lip
of a little dell shaded by beech trees. Caution had once
more ignored her name, for in their eagerness she and the

stablemaster had not ridden far. The turf was deep, and the two of them were too engrossed in one another to be aware of me as I halted my mount and stared down on them. Her discarded dress was like a wilted blossom on the grassy sward. She was so pale, a moon of a woman spread wide on his night-blue cloak, her head thrown back in ecstasy. She shuddered with each of his thrusts; his eyes were closed and his teeth showed white in his tanned face. Nearby, her mare grazed, heedless of them. But the Spotted Stud watched them so avidly that even he was unaware of me and my horse. When he fell forward atop her, head bowed in completion, she seized his face in both her hands and moved his mouth to hers to kiss him so passionately that I could not doubt her love for him.

Cold with dismay, I turned my horse's head and quietly withdrew. What I had seen sickened me. For I loved Queen-in-Waiting Caution and desired no harm or scandal to come her way. Had I not raised her, at the expense of my own childhood? Had I not stood at her side, shielded her from punishment and, as often as not, claimed her misdeeds as my own? Had I not offered her my own body for her pleasure, to help her to stay virginal for her wedding bed? If I had offered her my heart as well, then I had done so freely, knowing that she could never reciprocate what I felt. I had always accepted that in our relationship I must love her more than she loved me, for I was merely a servant, and she was a Farseer and would someday be queen of all the Six Duchies.

But it was him she chose. She loved the stablemaster, a man born a slave and a Chalcedean, not even an honest Buck-born servant like myself. To that common man she had given her heart and the body that I had cared for and cherished since she was born. Another might have felt jealousy, but I write the truth that Redbird bade me keep clear: I felt only fear for what might befall my darling.

And yes, I feared for myself as well. I knew that if my knowledge became public, I would fall just as swiftly as the princess, for although no one had ever said I was her chaperone, I knew that was what they had expected of me.

As soon as I was sure, I ran to my mother for advice, for she was at court in those days, nursemaid to Lady Everlon's twin daughters. Busy as she was, she still made time for me, and found a quiet place where I could spill out my tale of scandal and fear.

When I had told out my woe, my mother shook her head. "You must keep them apart," she counselled me, and when I said I could not, she scowled. "Then you must be ready. I will tell you the herbs you can mix with her drink that will make conception less likely, but none of them are certain. Sooner or later, if she is with the man, she will get with child. And if that happens, there is but one path for you. See that you, too, are quickening with life."

"But no man wishes to marry me!" I protested, and my mother shook her head.

"Learn what the Queen-in-Waiting knows. You do not have to be married to lie with a man. You do not even have to hold his heart. There are minstrels in plenty at the court, and all know that a minstrel will lie down with any woman for an hour, and play a sad song about her the next day. So choose one and ready him, so that if you need his services, he will be eager."

"But why?" I asked. "What will it avail me to be with child when my lady is?"

"Just do as I say, and all will be made clear with time," she told me. And then she shooed me from her chamber, for Lady Everlon had returned.

So I went, resolved that I would follow her advice, though I did not see the wisdom of it.

As the winter wore on, the Queen-in-Waiting did not rise as willingly from her bed as she once had. She turned aside from food, and the perfumes she had once loved now sickened her. She ceased going out to ride. I knew, I think, even before she suspected. I fled to my mother, and mixed with Caution's morning tea the herbs my mother gave me for shaking a child from the womb. So sick was the Queen-in-Waiting for the next week that I was certain the child must let go, and worried only that I had given my dear Caution too much of the remedy. Slowly she recovered and

I dared to hope, but when I dressed her hair, and when I smelled her skin as I slept beside her, I knew I was wrong. The child still clung within her and I dared not try to dislodge it again.

Her ladies began to whisper, and as the days passed and Caution puked at the sight of food and slept half the day away, the whispers rose to a roar. My best efforts to keep her safe had failed. The Queen-in-Waiting was with child and soon her symptoms were such that there was no hope of concealing it any longer. There came a day when her mother summoned her to a private audience, and when she returned silent and grey-faced, I knew that her mother had had the truth of her condition from her.

Some say this brought so much sorrow to her mother that she lay down and died. It is beyond me to know the truth of such things, but before the winter was out, Queen Capable was in her grave. This doubled the grief of King Virile. He rebuked his daughter, but Caution was unrepentant. Many a noble man offered to wed her, some even to let her keep the unborn child in her household. She refused them all. Nor would she name the father of her child, but when her nobles asked her, "Whose child is that which grows in your belly?" she would laugh almost wantonly and say, "Obviously, the child is mine. Cannot you see it grows within me?"

Then her duchies reproached her as well, dukes and duchesses all, saying, "Our Queen-in-Waiting you are, that

is true, but you are not yet our queen. Your father still holds the throne, and should he name another heir in your place, perhaps we would listen to him."

She stared round at them and with a grim smile replied, "My father knows I am his daughter. And any child that grows within me is his grandchild, and the rightful heir. He knows that. If you doubt that, you insult my mother's memory. Take that thought to my father and see how well it sits with him." Thus she made their doubts of her an insult to her mother, and knew her father would never hear them.

Yet for all her boldness in public, I knew that at night, when she thought I was asleep, she wept and berated herself for what had come to pass. Too late she had learned to follow her name, for though the stablemaster daily brought the Spotted Stud, saddled and bridled, to the courtyard, she did not go down to him, nor so much as wave her dismissal from a window. So every day he waited, an hour or sometimes two, and then he and the horses would return to the stables. Sometimes I peeped from the window to see him standing there patiently, holding the reins of our mounts and looking straight ahead.

To me alone, Caution spoke of her sorrows. She felt the loss of her mother keenly, even though they had not been close since she was a little girl. Her mother had always been the one to temper her father's anger and when he would have disciplined her more strictly, her mother had always intervened. King Virile's dark eyes were full of hurt when he looked at his daughter now, and the two of them seemed to avoid one another instead of being drawn together by their grief. So Caution felt her father was lost to her as well. Since her pregnancy had become known, Virile had asked his wife's younger sister to keep watch over his daughter and to regulate her conduct.

Lady Hope was as feisty as a yapping dog, and fully a match for my mistress's resourcefulness. That stern chaperone was never more than a few steps away from her charge, severely restricting her activities to those she considered appropriate. She might sew, or walk with her ladies in a garden, or listen to music. There was no hope of her going out to ride, even if she had felt well enough to do so. In the evenings, the key was turned in the lock to our suite of rooms, and two guards stationed outside it lest so much as a slip of paper be slipped beneath the door.

And so she pined for her lover as well as suffering the early trials of her pregnancy. I wondered if she had managed to convey to Lostler that she carried his child. She had not been out of my sight since my ill-fated attempt with the herbs, and sending him a secret note would have been useless, him being unlettered in any language. He would surely hear, though, of her disgrace. I hoped he would be wise enough not to try to contact her, for if he betrayed her secret, it would not go well for any of us.

Why no one else made the obvious connection, why her father did not dismiss the man or order him flogged, I did not understand. Perhaps a princess dallying with her stablemaster was too shameful a thing for him to imagine possible. Perhaps those who might suspect did not openly accuse Lostler for fear of deepening the Queen-in-Waiting's disgrace and earning the king's disfavour. Perhaps the king deluded himself that the child was nobly bred, if not legitimate, and that the father might yet step forward to claim his get. Or perhaps the death of his wife and his daughter's disgrace had so unmanned him that he had no heart left to solve such a sordid mystery. Daily it stabbed me that I had not been firmer with her, that I had let her fall into this disgrace.

And in another way I failed her. I was my mother's child, but seemed to lack both her nerve and her fecundity. I had dithered and delayed, hoping in vain that Caution would be done with the stablemaster before his seed took root in her. And then I told myself that my herbs would shake the child from her. Although I was the first to know she carried a child, still it was hard for me to choose a man to aid me in my plan likewise to conceive.

At last, in desperation, I settled on a man I thought I could seduce. Copper Songsmith was a young apprentice to the court. He was not as handsome then as he would grow to be, for he was wild-haired and gangly and had not yet seen a score of years, although even then he possessed a voice that made women swoon. I was not skilled in the ways of seduction and he was not a man expecting to be seduced. So we were both awkward at our task, and I at least was pretending to an ardency I did not truly feel. He was not a skilled lover and I did not care. Our matings were hurried and brief. When even after this my courses still came at their appointed time, I knew despair.

Again I sought my mother. She folded her lips tight and shook her head at my foolishness. "Well, what can you do but try again? If Eda favours you, then you may still get a lusty babe that will come early, or perhaps your lady may carry hers past term. But you had best be about it, and not be too fussy. What sort of a simpleton did I give birth to, a woman who cannot coax a man to settle between her legs?"

Her words stung, but it was advice I heeded. Before the next moon turned, I felt morning sickness. Being rid of Copper was no problem: at a hint that I might carry his child, his master whisked him off to Bearns Duchy for the winter, and I was glad to be shed of him. I did not at first tell my mistress what I had done. When the nights grew cold, and her worries pressed her, she still sometimes called me to her bed, not to take pleasure of me, but to lean her head on my shoulder and natter on about her secret love and how sorely she missed him.

Sometimes she spoke longingly of her lost freedom to take out the Spotted Stud on a long gallop and return in a leisurely fashion. Even then, she believed that I was ignorant of who her lover was. Such a fool she thought me! And so, not unknowingly of how it pricked me, she taunted me with hints of him, of the smoothness of the skin on his back, or the softness of his mouth when he kissed her. She spoke, too, of a hundred different plans for eluding her draconian chaperone, to slip away to be with her lover. Her plans were wild and foolish, yet when she hammered at me to agree to help her, what could I do but promise to aid her? Time after time she tried to set them in motion, and time after time I managed to delay her. She was growing both impatient and angry with me, and daily I feared she would attempt an escape that would end in disaster for us all. Her longing for him cut me deeper than she knew. And so, on the night that she first divined that I, too, was with child, I suddenly discerned a way to perhaps break her bond with the Chalcedean stableman and put an end to her plans for escape.

We were in bed together, cuddled close for warmth. Outside the shuttered windows of her bedchamber, a snowstorm was blowing fiercely. The wind whistled past the shutters and the flames of the hearth fire danced to their tune. Occasionally a blast struck with enough fury to send a ripple through the tapestries that lined the cold stone walls of the room. "Hold me, Felicity! The night is so chill," she whispered to me, and I was glad to comply. But she turned her face away from mine, exclaiming, "Your breath is foul with vomit! Are you ill?"

I shook my head and decided that night I would share my secret. "Only as ill as you are, my lady. The babe that grows inside me roils my belly."

"You?" She sat up in astonishment, letting the cold air of the room rush into our shared bed. "You with child?" She laughed aloud, but it was not a joyous sound. Her incredulous manner mocked me. "By whom?" she demanded, her mouth full of cold smiles. "What boy or gaffer did you waylay in a dark stairwell?"

I am not a beauty, nor even pretty. It is kind to say that I am plain. I am crook-toothed and thin-shanked and pock-faced. I know that the kitchen lads call me 'Pig eyes'. I cannot explain then why her mockery cut me so deep, save that she had never before spoken me so. Sometimes I look back and wonder, did she feel I had betrayed her? Had she secretly wished that my heart would always be hers and hers alone? Why else whet her tongue against me?

But I had been schooled to my place in her world for every day of my life. So even at that moment, no angry retort passed my lips. My plan to save her, and myself, sprang full-formed to my mind at that moment. So I only smiled, showing my crooked teeth and said, "Perhaps the stablemaster is not as keen of sight as others, for he did not seem to find me uncomely when he took me to warm his bed."

A thousand, a thousand-thousand times I have wished those words unsaid. They were the words that ended my life. My lady went red, and then white, so pale I thought she would faint. And then she whispered, in a voice as cold as a drowned man, "Go hence, Felicity. Sleep in your own bed tonight. Or in his. I've no need of you just now."

'Just now' she said, but her voice said 'any more'.

I left her bed and crossed the cold room, to enter my little chamber and clamber into my freezing bed. As I huddled there, sleepless, the rest of the night, I heard no weeping from her room. Only a terrible quiet.

I rose in the morning and went to tend her, but found her already up and dressed. Her face was white, her eyes set deep in dark circles. She did not stir from her room that day, nor say more than a dozen words to me. I brought her meals and took them away uneaten. I was pathetically grateful that she did not send me away entirely. My efforts to speak to her went unanswered, and she looked past me, but not at me. The pain of my lie cut me deep for the sorrow it had caused her. Yet I will not deny there was a satisfaction that although she might cut off all contact with Lostler over his supposed infidelity, her love for me, her humble and homely serving maid, was great enough that she did not rebuke me nor send me away. Every time I felt the urge to confess to her, I stifled it, thinking, 'She will get over her pain, and if I tell her, I will be the one she abandons. I have saved her from going to him, saved her from anyone discovering the truth.' Thinking this helped me to bear the pain of her exiling me from her thoughts.

Only to my mother did I admit my transgression, and she gave me no cause to doubt my impulse. Instead, she praised me warmly and whispered to me that I was far more clever than she had ever given me credit for. She also spoke urgently of all I had yet to do, saying that the moment the Queen-in-Waiting began to feel the surges of birth I must come to her and tell her. This I agreed to easily. She urged me, also, to mutter against Lostler to the other servants, saying that he had treated me badly in abandoning me once he knew I carried a babe, but this I did not have the courage to do. One lie surely was enough, and even then I suspected that the consequences of it might be deeper than I knew.

And so I continued to serve Caution faithfully, even if she kept me at a cool distance. I pretended that I thought it the result of her pregnancy, and was ever more solicitous of her comforts.

In the days that followed, Caution grew more silent and more wan. She spoke little and was without spirit. She ceased all efforts to defy her chaperone Lady Hope, but was as docile as a cow as she sat with her sewing untouched in her lap. She would not walk in the gardens, or descend to the Great Hall for music. Word of her bleak spirits spread through the court. At her command, many a visitor I turned away from her door. Finally, the king himself, his face lined with his grief, came to her. Him I could not turn away; instead, he sent me from her room, but I crouched on the floor by the door to my chamber and listened.

He did not comfort her with gentle words of forgiveness and encouragement. Instead, he spoke gravely, telling her that he knew she now realized how foolish she had been and what a grave error she had committed. He admitted to her that had she been his son, folk would have shrugged off her breach of conduct. But she was not and neither one of them could change that. Then he told her, bluntly, that many of his nobles had come to him asking that he set her and her unborn child aside as heir, and instead put the crown of King-in-Waiting on the raven locks of his young nephew Canny Farseer.

I peered through the crack to see her lift her head at those words. "And would you do that, Father?"

He was silent for a long time. Then he asked her, "What would your will be in this, Caution?"

She said nothing for so long that I, and probably her father, thought she would say it would be for the best if she stepped aside. I feared she had lost the spirit to claim a throne. Then she said, "I have lost so many things. My mother is gone; she will never dance at my wedding. If I ever wed, it will not be as the cherished virgin daughter that you hoped to celebrate. I have disappointed and shamed you. I have disappointed and shamed myself, to give my heart and body to a man who was worthy of neither. And I have cheated the child that grows within me; the babe will have no father to defend him, no name save my own, no future except what I can bestow." She took a deep breath and when she let it out, she squared her shoulders. "Father, please do not take my crown and future. Please let me show you that I can be worthy of both, and that I can rear a child who is worthy to carry the Farseer name and wear the crown of the Six Duchies."

For a time the king sat silently, thinking. Then he nodded slowly. He did not say a word after that, not even a farewell, but rose and left her chamber.

The next day, when she rose, she called me to her. She did not speak kindly or cruelly, but directed me to arrange a bath for her, scented with lavender, and to lay out an assortment of dresses that might still fit her well despite her belly, and to put out hose and low shoes and such jewellry as was of the best quality without being girlish. I hastened to obey her, with no complaint that she had given me all the work that half a dozen women would usually do for her. I felt only happiness that she seemed to believe I could do it all and well, and that she had not called her staff back to attend her.

Dressed and groomed, she descended. She ate in the Great Hall, where all might see and know that she had arisen from her gloom. She was subdued, but there was a fiery anger that glinted in her eyes. I wondered who would be the target for it, but when she made it known that she wished to call a general assembly of all the dukes, duchesses and lesser nobles then present at Buckkeep, I wondered no longer. She commanded, too, that the four senior minstrels attend, to witness and then to carry the account of the assembly out to the land. By this, I knew she had a plan, for to call such a council usurped her father's right to do so. It was the first time she had truly behaved as if she were a Queen-in-Waiting, calling upon the power that someday would be entirely hers.

When all the higher nobles then visiting Buckkeep were gathered, and all the lesser nobles present at the keep were standing in the audience hall, she stood up and said, "No king do I need now, or ever, to share my bed or my throne or even to get me a child. For I have these things already, bed, throne, and heir, and I shall never share them with any man. Have no doubt about the throne and the crown of the Six Duchies. I will be your queen, and my child will reign after me. I will not wed, and there will be no other children to challenge my child's claim. You have only to look at me to know that my child will be well born, taking from me the Farseer bloodlines that pass on the right to rule. No other heir could be named who could carry more of that bloodline than my child does. So be content with the heir that I will give to you. I need no husband and my child needs no father."

Although these furious words were intended for the ears of the aristocracy, she must have known that they would spread much farther than the walls of that room. Her nobles took her words to mean that a member of the nobility had fathered her child. As far as I know, she did nothing to correct that idea.

I doubt that the evening stars had appeared that winter day before Stablemaster Lostler had heard how little she needed or wanted him. I thought surely that he would find some way to contact her then. But either he did not or he failed in his attempt. Perhaps her abandonment of their meetings followed by this pronouncement that she needed no man cut his love at the root. Or perhaps he had never loved her at all. Perhaps he was relieved she did not name him nor seek him out. If what he had done to her had become common knowledge, there would have been only one fate for him.

I think perhaps Caution expected some sort of response from him. In the days that followed she seemed on edge, as if waiting for something. I would be about my tasks in her chambers and look up to find her staring at me, as if measuring my belly or comparing my form to hers to see why he might have wanted me. It was only later, when I looked back over that time, that I realized that she never doubted me. She never questioned me about my supposed tryst with her lover, never asked how many times I'd been with him or if he'd muttered fond words to me. She believed me. She trusted me.

I have to believe, then, that she loved me. Loved me more than she loved him, that she had such faith in my word. To my knowledge, she never even gave him the chance to claim he had been faithful to her. My hasty words had cut him from her heart.

Days turned to weeks turned to months. Time crawls and rushes with pregnancy. I was more aware of the Queen-in-Waiting's pregnancy than my own. Caution did not retire from court life, but plunged into it, yet not to dance and gamble and listen to the minstrels as she once had. Instead she applied herself to learning its inner workings. She began to have a care for where the supplies came from for the seamstresses and spinners, for the cooks and the warriors. Some few times she visited the judgment chambers and listened to her father solve disputes, but chiefly she involved herself in the domestic aspects of Buckkeep, and I think that pleased her father very much.

A few times I found her at her window, looking down on the courtyard and the stables beyond it. Lostler exercised the Spotted Stud daily, as he always had. I suspect he took great comfort in his beast companion, as those who have the Wit-magic do. She could not help but see him take the big stallion out. Once she caught me watching her and shrugged. "It is scarcely worth my while paying the keep for that beast now that I can no longer ride him. I should sell him at the next fair; I have read that it is good to change the stallions in a stable, to keep the breeding blood fresh." And I nodded but did not think she could ever bring herself to do it. Even then, I believed that sooner or later she would go down to her lover, find a way to have words with him, and that my deceit might be discovered. I dreaded it and feared it, but mostly I treasured every moment that I had her to myself again.

The winter turned to spring, and the babes in our bellies kicked and turned. The court seemed almost to have accepted the Queen-in-Waiting's solo production of an heir. There was gossip still and speculation and rumour, but they seemed to hold back their judgment of her. Her father, I know, was pleased with her more subdued air and her attention to the business of the keep, and perhaps her nobles were as well. At least, there was no more talk of replacing her. No noble youths came to court her any more, true, but it seemed to me that the more mature of her nobles now cast a considering eye on her, and I thought that, after the babe was born, she might find a different crop of suitors coming to call, despite her renunciation of any husband.

She carried the final months of her pregnancy well, for the morning sickness left her. She even began to go out and about, though only within the keep. She took tea with her ladies, and visited again the weaving and sewing rooms, and sat by the great hearth in the evenings with her ladies to hear the minstrels sing.

The Cattle and Horse Fair was always held in spring, and so it came that year. It scarcely seemed that it could have been a full two years since first she had beheld the Spotted Stud and his stuttering groom, and yet it was. It was one of her noble friends who artlessly reminded her of this, asking her if she would not go down in a pony cart to take in the sights of the fair that she had once so enjoyed. The Queen-in-Waiting, standing near her window, hand on her belly, had smiled bitterly and replied that she was far too heavy to contemplate even the short journey by cart to the fair. One of her ladies, thinking to be witty, asked if she did not wish to ride her Spotted Stud there. I could not be sure I heard a knife hidden in that question but I suspected one. I lifted my eyes from my sewing and looked directly at her, but the lady was smiling sweetly, with no hint of malice that I could see.

I saw Caution flinch at her question, and took that as my answer. It stung. Had she made that lady privy to a secret that she had not entrusted even to me? Or had the lady divined it on her own? It did not matter. Some knew, or at least suspected. Cold rose in my heart and the babe in my womb squirmed uneasily. It was a danger to my lady, one I could not ignore. I had been a fool not to see it earlier. Head bent over my sewing, I looked through my lashes around the room at her gathered women. Some were there who had never before been in her circle.

Of course.

Anyone party to such a secret, anyone who asked a pointed question might then use that knowledge as a lever to raise her social standing. It pained me to see Caution like a stag surrounded by slavering hounds. I vowed to myself that I'd do all I could to see her not pulled down. I seethed in meek silence, wishing to kill them all.

But first, I must deal with the stablemaster. He and his Spotted Stud must be sent away, banished to somewhere he could never, by word or look, betray the Queen-in-Waiting. If I had been a man, perhaps I would have thought of ways to kill him. But I was a woman and guile is a woman's best weapon, my mother had always taught me. And so I waited until the next morning when she was looking out the window and sighing to herself as Lostler stood in the stableyard and groomed the Spotted Stud.

No other ladies were present, and I placed myself at her elbow and said softly, "I know it grieves you to look on that beast and know you cannot ride him. Soon you will be a mother and after that, eventually, the queen of all the Six Duchies. I know you can see he is no longer a fitting and proper mount for you. You should sell him now, just as you bought him. Send him out of your life and out of your thoughts. Once he is gone, you will not have to look at him and remember your wild adventures with him."

I spoke so carefully, and looked only at the horse, but I knew how she would hear my words. I felt her hesitation as she said, "Perhaps I should."

So I pushed her to the deed. "The horse fair lasts but another three days. Be decisive, my queen. Send him hence, out of your life. Let no one see your regrets, and others will recognize your strength in setting him out of your life. They will see that truly you are ready to bestride a throne instead of a Spotted Stud." She was still silent and staring, but her hurt showing in her glistening eyes. I had to push harder. "Let everyone see you stand alone and strong, needing no one else to make your decisions for you."

She glanced at me, and then her eyes fell to my belly. She clenched her lips in a flat line and said nothing. A moment later, she resolutely crossed the room to a bell-pull, and summoned a page. Her words were terse. "I have decided to sell the Spotted Stud at the horse fair. He shall go to the first bidder, regardless of the offer. We have plenty and more than enough of his get at Buckkeep. It is time to send him away. I wish him taken there immediately."

The boy bowed. "I shall tell the stablemaster immediately."

The Queen-in-Waiting shook her head. "No. Do not bother him with it. He will argue and it is a decision I have already made. Have the keep's smith take him away right now. Tie him to the tail of a cart and take him down to the market grounds. He cannot fight his way free of that."

"As you wish, your highness."

The boy departed and Caution returned to the window to stand and watch.

Now, the smith was a man with little love for Stablemaster Lostler. He was the brother of the stablemaster the Queen-in-Waiting had dismissed, and so he harboured a grudge against the man who had taken his brother's position and livelihood. All knew this. And so when the page brought the word to him, I am certain the man did not delay, but set aside his hammer and hung up his apron and brought his heavy smithy cart around to the stableyard.

We saw him pull up his cart and stride into the stables. He carried a heavy length of chain. He was a massive man, tall as well as heavily muscled. Lostler had put the stud back in his stall and was working with a young bay filly in the exercise yard. The smith did not pause to speak to him. We were high above the stables, but even so, the stallion's scream of fury reached us. Caution leaned forward on the stone sill, staring out, her eyes wide in her pale face, her mouth set. Hurt warred with the satisfaction of revenge on her features. I saw what she strove to do. She would sell Lostler's Wit-companion, tear from him that which he loved as she believed he had torn her love for him.

There was a second scream from the horse, and we saw Lostler call hastily to a groom who came to take the mare from him. The stablemaster turned and ran back into the stables. For three breaths, all was calm below us. The groom began to lunge the mare, a stablehand approached the door with a barrow full of feed, while two young stableboys, brooms on their shoulders, followed him in.

But a moment later, the boys and the man with the barrow came scrambling back out. We heard shouts and saw men running both toward and away from the stables. A moment later, locked together, Lostler and the smith emerged. The smith was dragging Lostler by his shirt front. The stablemaster's face was bloodied, but he was still fighting, landing blow after blow on the impassive smith. We could hear the stallion's angry screams from inside the stable. The smith drew the stablemaster up to his full height, struck him a tremendous blow in the face and then dropped him disdainfully into the dust. Lostler fell bonelessly to the earth. The smith did not even look down at him, but strode back into the stable.

And Caution's resolution failed her. "Lostler! No! What have I done?" she wailed as she stared down at the man's still body. And then, moving more swiftly than she had in weeks, she spun away from the window and ran across the room. She was out the door while I was still staring after her. By the time I reached the hall, she was halfway down the stairs, running as no pregnant woman should. "My queen, mind your child!" I called after her, but she did not pause. And so I gathered my skirts and went after her, hampered by my own heaviness.

I was not as swift as she was. I was out of breath by the time I reached the bottom of the stairs. The best I could manage was a brisk walk, but when I heard her screams, I gritted my teeth and ran again. I pushed past other servants hurrying to see what the commotion was. By the time I emerged into the stable yard, a crowd had gathered. I shoved my way recklessly through the useless, shouting crowd, and still arrived too late.

I cannot say what had gone before. I saw the Spotted Stud, blood pouring from his chest as he reared to the sky, hooves flailing. He screamed, but it sounded like more anguish than pain. The Queen-in-Waiting, her hands lifted defensively against the stallion's attack, cowered in the mud by the stablemaster's body. He was dying. She had

tried to gather his body into her lap but his hands reached toward the Spotted Stud. As he fell back against her, dead or dying, I saw the unfurling rose of blood that was blossoming on his chest. Something had stabbed him; his blood was a bright-red rose on the breast of his pale shirt. The smith stood over the Queen-in-Waiting, between her and the infuriated Spotted Stud, pitchfork in his knotted hands, stout legs braced for the next attack. Blood reddened the tines of the fork.

My mind leaped to the conclusion: the horse had attacked and he had fended it off, and then defended himself against the stablemaster. As I watched in horror, the horse came down as the man thrust up. The fork sank deep into the stud's chest, and then the animal tore it free of the smith's grip as he fell forward onto it. The handle of the fork struck the smith a terrible blow. With a final scream, the dying stallion collapsed less than an arm's length from Caution. Blood fountained from his wounds and blew out on his fading scream. Gouts of his blood, from both his black hide and his white, leaped onto her dress, wetting her to the very skin. At that touch, she shrieked as if scalded, and fell onto Lostler's breast as if to shield him.

The blood blotched her with scarlet. The horse bared his teeth and then sank down, dead, his muzzle touching his master's lax hand. Half in Caution's lap, Lostler suddenly sagged, as lifeless as his horse. Stablemaster and Spotted Stud were both dead.

Sounds ebbed to one instant of silence, then rose in a roar of shrieks, shouts and exclamations. But I heard only the Queen-in-Waiting's shrill scream, which went on and on and stopped only when she crumpled, senseless, spattered and soaked with blood from both horse and man.

"Get back, let me through!" I was shrieking, but no one heeded me. They all surged forward like hounds ringing a kill, and I was pushed back and to one side. I could not so much as touch the dripping hem of her skirt as she was gathered up and carried back toward the doors.

As I could not get close to her there, I thought to be clever and forced my aching legs to hurry ahead of the throng and run up the stairs to her chambers. Surely they would bring her there, I thought, and I would be waiting. But they didn't. The fainting Queen-in-Waiting was borne off, at the king's command, to her mother's chambers, adjacent to his own. The king's own healer was summoned to attend her. By the time I realized my error and went there, a dozen other ladies had won entrance before me. I could scarcely get close to the door, but the muttered gossip I heard shocked me. When they had stripped the bloodied clothing from her body, they had discovered that some of it was hers. Queen Caution had awakened from her faint calling for the stablemaster, and then gasping in pain as the sudden cramps took her. In the midst of her grief, her child was struggling to be born.

I fled to my mother.

I think she was waiting for me. Her latest ward was asleep, but she had kept to the room where she had put him down. The hearth fire burned quietly, snapping and muttering to itself. A pot of tea, freshly made, steamed beside it. The babe's mother had rushed off to join in the general clamor about the Queen-in-Waiting, so we were alone when I sank to the floor beside my mother's chair and leaned my head against her knee. "It was terrible," I said. "They have taken her from me and I don't know what to do."

My mother jerked her knee away from me. "Stop being stupid. That's the first thing, Felicity." I straightened up and stared at her. Against my will, tears filled my eyes at her harsh tone. She ignored them. "I wish you had listened better to me before, but there is no time to rebuke you now. Sit up, listen, and do as I say: you may yet have a chance to keep your position, and perhaps find a better life for the child you carry."

She arose from her chair and stepped away from me. I stood more slowly and followed her as she went to her clothing chest and opened it. From the corner of it, she took a small cloth bag and pushed it into my hand. It weighed nearly nothing. "I prepared this for you two months ago," she told me proudly. Clearly she expected me to be grateful. "Brew it as a tea and drink it quickly. Do not allow yourself to vomit it up, no matter how your stomach heaves. As soon as you feel your pains begin, come to me, here, and I myself will deliver your child in my room. There we will keep him or her safe and quiet and unsuspected for now. Then will come your time to be brave and strong. For you must arise from the birth bed, pad your belly out as if you still carry a child, and find a way to gain access to Caution.

"Do not fear that she will deliver her child before yours is born. No matter how hearty they seem, the high-born ones always make much of pushing out a babe, as if they were the very first one to ever do so, or as if there were some great talent to it. She will take her time. Your task will be to get to her side and to remain, as you ever have been, her first and most reliable servant."

I was gaping at her. When I found breath to speak, I asked, "Why? Why must my child be born this day, and why must I conceal it from everyone?"

She looked at me as if I were simple. "If I did not know you were mine, I would think an idiot mothered you!" she snapped. "There are two paths opening before you. You must be ready for them. The first is that you must be in milk when the new prince or princess is born, so that you can be the wet-nurse for the child. You have the right to that position, and you must not let it be snatched away from you. And the second..."

She lowered her voice and beckoned me closer, speaking in a whisper. "All new-born babes look alike. I will tell you that is true, no matter what anyone says. As they grow, they may reflect the looks of their mother or father or both. But in this situation, no one save the Queen-in-Waiting is in a position to say what the father of her child looked like. And thus, when you carry off one infant to nurse, and return to put another in his place, no one will be the wiser."

I stared at her, trying to order her words to make sense. "What child?" I asked, even as the immensity of what she suggested dawned on me.

"Your child, stupid girl. My grandchild. If the gods favour us, your babe will match the sex of the Farseer heir. You will whisk her babe away, to wash and nurse it. And you will bring back to her a tidy, well-wrapped child who will someday sit on the throne of the Six Duchies."

"But why?"

"Why not?" she snapped. "What silliness says that a child born to this woman is born to be a king, and the child of that woman born to grub in a field? Why not lift a seed of our family to be a king or queen? We will keep the secret and you will raise your own babe, gowning him in silk and wrapping him in furs. Someday, when he is old enough to possess the secret, you will tell him that which he will know he must keep private. And then you, and I and your father and your siblings will live more generously than ever we have before, partaking of the largesse of a royal heir. Don't you see, my dear Felicity? All is within our grasp, if only you are bold enough. I stepped forward and changed your life for you, as the cost of giving you up. Now you can take the next step. Put your child on a throne."

She made it sound so simple. My mind chased itself in circles. As I sat, transfixed by her words, she shook her head at me and snatched the little bag of herbs from my hand. She refilled her cup of tea, dumped in the contents of the little bag, and stirred it well. We were silent as it steeped. When she handed it to me, I asked her, "And what will become of Caution's child?"

"We will pass it off as yours, of course," she said. Then, as I took my first sip of the brew she handed me, she added, "At first. He cannot be raised near Buckkeep, of course, in case the resemblance is too pronounced. If he is healthy enough, we have a cousin in Tilth who will foster him for us."

I took another swallow. I had expected it to be bitter. It was not. It was aromatic, almost pleasant. "I've never heard that I had cousins in Tilth."

She shook her head impatiently. "There is much you do not know, raised so much away from me. Drink it down

quickly now, all at once. Then, go back to your chambers and make sure all is ready for the Queen-in-Waiting's child. Do not vomit. The pains will start soon enough. Come to me then, and not before."

I did as she told me. She was correct in every way. My belly soon wished to be rid of her brew, but I clenched my teeth and would not gag. And when the pains started, I hurried back to her. I had seen women in labor, and been present at a birth or two that Caution had also attended. I knew how it should go, the slow increasing of the cramp and the gradual readying of woman's body. This was not like that. Whatever my mother had given me rushed my body through the process. She had prepared everything for me, in the little room that was her own. There was water, and rags in plenty, and a blanket in which to wrap the child. She came and went as I gasped my way through my birthing. She had commanded me to silence, so I bit on a twist of rag to hold in my screams. Finally my little son was born in a gush of water and fluid, and my mother exclaimed in dismay at the sight of him.

"What's this?" she demanded of me, as if she had asked for meat and I'd given her fish. "So tiny! And look at his hair! Reddish gold! What were you thinking, girl? The Queen-in-Waiting's hair is black and so is the stable-master's, just like yours. Could not you find a dark-haired man to lie down with you?"

I was still panting with the effort of birthing him and had little patience for her rebuke. "If I had known the ruse you intended," I began, but when I saw her eyes narrow in fury, I simply said, "Let me see him."

"Soon enough," she replied, setting my boy aside. "Clean yourself first and pad your belly a bit. You must be on your feet and back by Caution's side as quickly as you can. As soon as you're ready, we'll let him suckle a bit to bring your milk in. But now is no time to linger here. Who knows our luck? It may be that the Queen-in-Waiting's child will be unremarkable, and no one at court knows who the father was. You may yet be able to make the switch."

I listened to her. As I always had. Sometimes it seems odd to me that a mother so little present in my life could command me so, and at other times it seems that I had had so little of her that of course I would take of her whatever I could get. Perhaps if I had loved the baby's father, perhaps if I had anticipated his birth with joy, then I would have felt differently. But, strange to say, I had always thought more of Caution's baby than my own, always wondered if her child would carry too much of the father's features. So when at last my mother handed me my bundled child and commanded me to give him suck, it simply seemed another task I must learn to do. I felt no wonder over his tiny hands or wisp of reddish hair. Instead, I saw how small he was.

I put him to my breast, and he suckled a little, and then almost immediately fell asleep. "Don't let him do that," my mother warned me and gave him a little jostle so that he opened his eyes. He nursed for a slightly longer time, then again dozed off.

"He doesn't seem very hearty," I said hesitantly. I feared she would rebuke me.

"Well, he isn't," she said bluntly. "You were late at your task, and so he's had to come early. Another month in the womb would have been better for him, but I've seen smaller children survive. He'll sleep a lot and you'll have to pinch him a bit to get him to nurse well. Here. Give him to me. I've plenty of milk still. And you have somewhere else to be."

She took my child and in my hand put a nosegay of flowers. She smiled proudly. "While you were getting ready to push him out, I went to the Women's Garden. Those will win you a place at the Queen-in-Waiting's side. It's an old remedy. Tell the women that you must hold them for her to breathe their fragrance between pangs. They will strengthen her. Now, off you go. And remember that I loved you enough to do all this for you."

I left her. Her words echoed an old memory.

As I trudged away from her room and then down the endless stairs, my body ached all over and all I longed to do was sleep. Instead, I was thinking of how I would get in to see Caution and wondering how her labor progressed. I knew she had not had her child yet. When she did, every horn and drum in the castle would sound, and riders would be sent out to each of the other duchies. I clutched my flowers and prayed they would let me in. And I thought of my own child not a bit. Only later did that seem odd to me, that although I had felt him grow and move inside me, he had never seemed real to me at all.

It looked as if the entire female populace of Buckkeep Castle had convened on the stairs and in the hall outside the Queen-in-Waiting's chamber. The signs among the gossiping knots of women were ominous. Hair had been loosened and sashes, too; and the laces of gowns and shoes were all undone and dangling. My heart caught and then surged painfully on. I knew what it meant. Caution was having a hard time giving birth. I hesitated on the stairs, and then a maid bearing a cushion with a gleaming knife on it hurried past me. I gasped and fell in behind her, carrying my bouquet before me as if we were both part of the same errand. The clustered women parted to let us pass, falling silent as we did so and then filling the air with whispers in our wake. As if by magic, the heavy wooden doors to the old queen's bedchamber opened before us. The king's men who guarded it lifted their crossed spears to let us pass. Unchallenged, I followed her in.

There were three midwives in the room, all wearing white aprons and with their sleeves rolled back. One was an old woman enthroned in a chair at the foot of the curtained bed. Of Caution I could see nothing, and heard only her harsh panting. The second midwife was a woman of middle years who bustled up to take both knife and cushion from the maid. She handed it off to the youngest, a matronly woman of at least thirty years. She dropped to her knees by the bed and carefully pushed the pillow and knife under the bed, promising, "This will cut your pain, my dear. A knife under the bed never fails to ease it."

The second midwife seemed to notice me abruptly. "Who let you in?" she demanded, advancing threateningly on me. "Who are you?" The other two closed ranks like guards, blocking me from the bed.

"I am Queen-in-Waiting Caution's handmaid, as I have been since her infancy. And long has it been promised to me that I should be wet-nurse for her child as well." I lied with wild abandon. I would have claimed to be the king if I had thought it would win me a way to her side. I heard her long groan of building pain. My poor Caution suffered. Then, "Lostler," she hissed, heedless of who might hear her agonized cry. "Lostler!" she said, more loudly, and then, as all three midwives bustled back to the curtained bed, "Lostler!" she shrieked, a drawn-out scream of physical pain and heartfelt anguish.

Her pain tore through me, slicing a new torment of my own. For she cried out for him, the man who had caused her all this trouble, rather than me, who had always helped her. Nevertheless, I held up in my shaking hands the nosegay of flowers my mother had prepared for me and said, "For long and long, the women of my family have suckled the children of the nobility. Many old cures are known to us, and I hold in my hands one that will ease her pain and help her bring her child into the world."

The old midwife scowled at me: well did I know of her long rivalry with my mother. I had heard her say that cows should not give themselves airs in regards to matters beyond their knowledge, but she did not so disparage me now. She had no opportunity. Caution had overheard my words, and she whispered harshly, "Bring me the flowers now, please, for I die of the pain, I die!"

Now the midwife could not dare to challenge my right to be there. I rushed to her side and held the flowers where Caution could smell them. She lifted both her hands and seized my wrists so tightly that to this day, I swear I can still feel that clutch. And the nosegay seemed to work its charm, for she seemed to gain strength for her task. She still cried out for Lostler at each pain, but the word ceased to seem a name and more like her rallying cry. I stayed by her side, and let her strangle my hands as she would. My own belly ached and I felt my womb tighten over and over, almost in time with hers. I knew this to be normal and even a good thing when it followed birth, but I could not shake the feeling that I labored alongside her, and that somehow my contractions aided hers.

She gained strength, it is true, but still she labored far longer than I liked. The midwife whispered to her assistants that she might have to cut the child from the Queen-in-Waiting's womb, or else risk losing both of them. At that, my mistress opened wide her eyes.

"No knife shall touch me!" she proclaimed. "Let my child come out as he went in. Enough blood has been shed over him!"

And all who were near gasped at her words, but none defied her, for all know that in this, the woman has the final say. And so she labored on, though I think the pain would have been less had she allowed the midwife to open her belly for the child's passing. Night gave way to dawn and then morning. Time and again the king sent messengers to her door, and over and over they were turned back with "not yet". Finally he sent a page to sit in the hall outside the door and wait. With the passing of the darkness, I saw my mistress weakening.

And when finally the midwife cried out, "I see the crown! A few more pushes, my queen, and your child will be here!" I saw her face whiten suddenly. Even her lips seemed pale as they pulled back from her teeth and I saw that she did not wait for her body, but pushed with every last bit of strength she had. The baby came then, in a final rush of blood and fluid, head emerging and then his body sliding out almost at once. The midwife caught him and held him up as joyously as if he were a fresh-caught salmon. "A boy!" she cried. "The Farseer line has a new prince! Send the runner to the king, and let the news reach his ears first, that he be the one to proclaim it!"

At once, one of her assistants rushed for the door. The other accepted the prince into a clean white blanket and began to gently rub him clean while the midwife awaited the afterbirth. It came in time and once that last push was done, Caution closed her eyes for a long time. Yet still she gripped my wrists between her hands and I did not move for fear of disturbing whatever small rest she might be finding. The midwife busied herself between the Queen-in-Waiting's legs, muttering her dislike of something. Cloth after cloth she folded and pressed there, and then pulled Caution's thighs close together and bound them in a wrapping. And then she turned to her assistant, who had been tugging at her sleeve and whispering at her for some time.

By then my mistress had begun to shake with cold, for she had labored long and now the heat of her work was leaving her. Blankets had been warmed by the hearth, and these were brought to her. When her shaking subsided, she demanded, "Where is my son? You have not yet shown him to me! Give him to me!"

I saw the look that passed between the assistant and the midwife. The midwife folded her lips and gave a sharp nod. The woman approached the Queen-in-Waiting hesitantly, made a deep curtsey and then offered her the bundled child.

Caution took him, smiling wearily, but as she lifted the flap of blanket to look into his little face, she exclaimed, "What is this clumsiness! You have not cleaned him! He is covered still in my blood. Look how it clings to his face!"

The midwife did not speak. Not from her lips ever came those tidings. It was the assistant who said, "May it please my queen, your son is as he is marked, red and white, piebald as a puppy."

"It pleases me not!" Caution cried wildly. "Wash him! Wash him clean for me!"

And then it was that I took the babe from her hands, and undid his wrappings that we might look on him. But it was as the midwife's aide had said. He was mottled with red splotches that stood up from his pale flesh. The midwife said in a low voice, "Many things can happen to mark a child. A fright, or a strong emotion of any kind. My queen, look on him, and see if the marks on his body do not match where the blood from that evil horse stained you as he died."

"No," Caution said. She looked down at her blotched babe, with half his face white and fair and half his face stained red. And then, "NO!" she shrieked and then her head fell back on her pillows and she fainted.

The midwife and her assistants bustled close to her side, pushing me away from her. I stepped back, cradling her child to my breast, and as if he knew that this was our fate, he turned his face toward me and quested for a nipple.

In the days that followed, I heard many a wild tale. Some said that the babe was so marked because his father was one in spirit with the Spotted Stud. Just as every foal born to the Spotted Stud's service was born with his spots, so must every child born to the beast's Wit-partner be likewise blotched. And others said that the baby had been marked in Caution's womb with the blood spattered on her, and it did not seem to make a difference whether it was Lostler's blood or the Stud's.

However it was, this I know for truth: Caution would never let the child be put to suck on her, and so from that moment he was mine to nurse. The Queen-in-Waiting lingered until the change of the moon, speaking little and always looking at me with accusing eyes whenever I came into the room. I knew she blamed me and I would take that blame with me to my grave. The only lie I ever told her was my undoing, and hers, and the stablemaster's. Such is the power of a lie given to one you love. And never did I think of telling her the truth, for I knew it would only make her lover's end more bitter in her memory, and that she would blame herself as well. That burden I kept from her and made it mine alone.

My queen never grew stronger, but dwindled away with that last moon until, in the dark of the moon, she died. My heart shrank as her spirit grew smaller, and when she died, something in me died as well. I cut my hair to mourn her, shearing it off shorter than even the king cut his. My mother rebuked me for this, and I heard gossip hissing and sputtering whenever I passed, but I cared nothing then for any of them or what they thought of me. My queen, my sister, my daughter, my lover, all were gone, as if the sun had vanished from the sky, leaving me with nothing but two squalling children.

I was as good a cow as my mother before me, with ample milk, and that was well, for my mother refused to nurse either child. "What future is there in giving suck to a bastard once his protector is dead?" she asked me bluntly. And coming close to me, she added quietly, "But there might be some who would reward a woman who saw that the king's bastard grandson did not prosper."

And that was when I took both infants from my mother's rooms and placed them in my own. And little enough did I have to do with her after that, or she with me. As if all that had come to pass were my own fault, she treated me. And perhaps it was true. And in times to come, when she could neither bear nor nurse, and thought that I would be the one to cushion her life, I did not. Nor do I regret that.

All seemed content to leave the boy to me, so I had his full care as well as my own son's. The little prince was hearty and strong. His face was mottled and his body as well, but no other flaw did he have to him. His eyes were bright and he nursed with an appetite.

Not so my own child. Born too soon, he was small and where some might have called him placid, I saw him as listless. The prince was pink and plump, but my child was sallow and sunken-eyed. Put to the breast, he dozed off too soon, and had to be pinched awake to nurse. He had not the spirit to cry loudly, but whimpered only. He slept well only when I put him down beside the prince, and so I did, for there was no one who cared enough to say that was not fitting.

In the days after his grandson's birth, the king was beside himself with grief. He had no thought to the grandson that remained to him, but only to the daughter he had lost. After four days, I named the boy Charger, for he needed a name, and it seemed a good name for a prince. But by then I was too late. The Piebald Prince was how the servants spoke of him. I went to the king himself with the infant, claiming that his mother had chosen that name and it was only proper that he be known by it. So he was entered as Charger Farseer on the rolls of Buckkeep. But since he was a bastard, no one bothered to seal that name to him, and few called him by it. And to the name Piebald he would answer to the end of his days.

Part Two

The Piebald Prince

To my natural son, I gave the name Redbird, for his hair was russet as a robin's breast feathers. He was smaller than Prince Charger, and not a healthy child at first. His vision was weak, so he developed a peering expression, and this I think was the result of him being forced so soon into the outer world. I raised him beside the prince, just as I had been raised beside his mother, but to my boy I did not give the ill counsels my mother had bestowed on me.

I requested a room on a higher floor than I had previously occupied, and the house steward was quick enough to find one for us. No one tried to take the bastard prince from me and if anyone even knew I had borne a child as well, no one cared. So it was that I lived on the floor above the royal family's quarters, but on a level below that occupied by the common servants. My neighbors were those well born, but not royal, and visiting nobility. I lived quietly among them. The court was happy to forget us.

I saw to the young prince's needs as I once had to his mother's, visiting the royal seamstresses when he needed new garments, and making sure that they were well made enough that they would serve my smaller son as well when he grew into the Charger's cast offs. As the months passed my son grew healthier, though he never matched his royal companion in size or appetite, and once he passed his sickly beginning, was an easy child, content to give way to the prince in all things. I mourned my lost princess and cherished her son for he was all I had left of her; but as the months passed, the razor of my pain dulled.

At Buckkeep life and politics must continue, no matter whose wife or daughter dies. In less than a year King Virile had been bereaved of both wife and daughter. Many said that he would follow them swiftly to the grave, for grief and shame as heavy as that might kill any man. They began to look to his younger brother, wondering if Virile would not name him as King-in-Waiting now. But in truth, King Virile bore up under his sorrows. I do not mean that I was privy to the king's private thoughts or doings, but only that I saw what everyone did. He still came to sit in judgment on the appointed days. The flesh of his face sagged with grief and his eyes were never clear, but he was clean and walked as tall and sat as straight as ever he had.

He became a man both grave and thoughtful, seldom smiling and never laughing, but a better king all the same than he had been in the years before his grief. For the next two decades, he was to rule wisely and well. At first, his dukes and duchesses spoke amongst themselves, saying: "Perhaps he will take another wife and get another heir for the

throne, for he is not too old a man to father another child, or even five." But the years came and went, and he showed no sign of this. Then they began to say, "Then surely he will name his brother's son, Canny Farseer, as heir to the Farseer throne." Many a noble daughter was presented to Canny Farseer as a suitable wife, with many a parent thinking that the daughter they placed before him now might sit upon the Farseer throne later.

Of the Piebald Prince little was noised about outside the castle at Buckkeep. Yet the truth of it must be told, even if minstrels have lied and said he was a twisted little half-man, wicked in his lies and cruel to his nurses. The truth makes a shorter tale: Charger was both as handsome and as ugly a child as has ever walked the earth. He was well made in form and in manner, save for the blotching of his flesh, and this discolouring was over his whole body, not just his face. For all the discolouration, his features were Farseer, resembling both his mother and his grandfather far more than his father. As for his temperament, he was as stubborn as his mother in having his own way, and near as silent as his father. For though it was seldom whispered, no one now doubted that Lostler the stablemaster had sired the boy.

Now this was the manner of his marking: the left side of his face was coloured as anyone might expect it to be. The right was blotched the colour of an over-ripe berry, from brow to chin, but not around his mouth. His hair was black, and dark brown his eyes. At the nape of his neck another blotch began, and trickled like spilled wine over his left shoulder. On his left arm, he was marred with three blots, and one was shaped like a bird with outstretched wings. On the back of his right leg the colour went from the back of his thigh to just below his knee. Now some will say that the splotches of colours were just the same as the Spotted Stud wore, as like to the places on the horse as a man's body can be. But by the time this was noised about, the horse was long dead, and man's memory is a chancy thing when the evidence is not before his eyes. So as to the truth of that, I will not vouch. I think it more likely that the blood of the stableman and the stallion had soaked the princess and marked the babe in her womb. For such things do happen, as is well known.

I had the raising of him for his infancy. And when the day came that Charger and Redbird could sit and listen, I was the one who took him, and my own boy beside him, down to the hearth in the Great Hall where the children took their lessons from Scribe Willowby. Even then, the law was that no child in Buckkeep could be denied learning, so no one thought to turn away either bastard, royal or red. And Willowby, being a just man, soon perceived that the Piebald Prince had a quick mind. The scribe himself appealed to the king for a proper tutor for the boy. I feared then that he would be taken from me, and my son and I turned out to find a new livelihood. But instead, when the boy was moved down the stairs to a set of rooms on the same floor as the king, Redbird and I joined him there, likely because they were empty and no one thought to forbid us from doing so.

Now, from the beginning, Charger had from his father the tongue of the beasts. This was a magic that in those days some folk owned to having with no shame, for at that time the degradations it might lead to were not well known. So folk would openly claim the Wit, and some made their living from having it, as huntmasters and beast-healers and swineherds and the like, and the Piebald Prince had the Wit in plenty. Humans might shun the patches that marred his face and body, but not beasts. They came to him as bees to nectar. Birds came through the windows to perch on the edge of his cradle. This is a truth I will swear to, for I saw it myself. There was no lapdog that would not leave its master's side to run at the boy's heels. Cats trailed after him. As he grew, there was not a horse in the stable he could not ride. All of this, he accepted as his due.

He was as well taught as a prince should be for, as he grew, the king himself saw to that, personally choosing his tutors, seeing that he learned his languages from those who had spoken them from birth and that he learned his history from a minstrel trusted to teach the boy the truth. Charger remained an apt and eager student. My Redbird was not so eager for his studies, and yet I insisted, switch in hand, that he be as attentive to the prince's lessons as if the tutor were his own. And so he learned.

Charger remained without noble friends of his own age or elders sympathetic to him. Instead, he found his friends as my Redbird did, amongst the lowly folk of the keep, the dog-boys and the kitchen-help and the gardeners and such. Redbird was ever at his heels, faithful as a hound, and often the two would fall asleep by the hearth, leaning on one another. Folk shook their heads to see any kind of a prince, even a piebald bastard one, reduced to such playmates.

In due time, Charger was tested for the Skill, and found to have little of the rightful Farseer magic. It was only with the greatest effort that the Skillmaster could reach his mind with his thoughts, and Charger was completely unable to make his own thoughts known to any of the king's coterie. Now some will say that this alone was a strong sign of his common birth, and others that the lowly magic of animals destroyed any Farseer magic in him. But no one can know one way or another, and therefore no proper minstrel would vouch for the truth of it. I would say that his mother had little ability for that magic either, and it is well known that it is not bestowed every generation, nor that every child of royal blood inherits the same strength of it.

King Virile ruled well and the Piebald Prince grew as boys will, sprouting up like bean plants, so that it seemed one but turned around and he stood one day as tall as his grandfather. By then my own Redbird, slight as he was, had been discovered to have a sweet voice and strong lungs. He had his father's looks, his copper hair and hazel eyes, and from his father too, he took his fine voice. More than once I overheard folk marvel that a rangy cow like me should have dropped such a fine calf. He would remain small of stature and slender as a boy for all his life, but he was sunny-natured, and clever at his letters and numbers. He was as cautious as the prince was daring, well aware he could not climb, wrestle or run as well as the other lads of his age; but for all that, he was utterly devoted to the prince, and for his part, Charger watched out for him as if he were a younger brother, with both fondness and tolerance for his lesser strength. I dared to dream large dreams for my son, but kept them to myself, resolved that he should be the one to steer his life.

When the minstrels of the keep offered to vouch for Redbird to enter their guild, he beseeched me to allow it. It cut like a knife but I smiled and I let him go. I told myself that it was right to let him have his own life. And he did not go far, for in those days his own father, Copper Songsmith, had returned to the keep. Although he never claimed Redbird as his son, he was pleased to take him as an apprentice. So I saw my son often enough, even if he did leave Buckkeep Castle to live in the Guild Hall with the other apprentices. Redbird chose to take the path of one who keeps the records and witnesses to the truth of agreements. He had many lineages to learn, and all of the old histories to memorize, but these things he seemed to relish. I sometimes thought of the days when only a switch would make him sit down and take heed, and wondered where that distractible child had gone.

So that left me tending a prince who needed less and less of my attention each day. I wondered what would become of me when he left my care, for I had not followed my mother in her career as a wet-nurse. Redbird remained my sole child, and I had small chance of bearing another who might bring me to milk again. My association with Caution and then her bastard had left its marks on me in many ways. My only unguarded friendships were those I had formed with the keep youngsters, mostly common, who had been the young playmates of the prince and my son. Those not restrained by their parents had been happy to frequent our chambers for stories and games. And as they grew, even if their parents did disapprove, I kept their regard. But a young man does not need a nanny forever.

When the time came for the prince to be given apartments of his own, I did not beg his mercy. And yet he granted it to me. He himself went to the king and asked that for my long service to him, I be given a chamber on the servants' floors and a small allowance for my needs. The king granted it. I wondered if he remembered my long service to his daughter as well, and if that had been in my favour or not. But I was in no position to question it and was grateful for what I got. And I was able to earn both coins and goodwill outside of that allowance through the care of small children for busy servants who did not wish to resign their positions to raise their own children. And so I remained at Buckkeep, and at least three times a week Prince Charger would call on me, often with my son at his side, for despite the differences in their stations the two remained close friends.

The prince was a lad of thirteen when King Virile began to summon him to duties as a page. He had gained his grandfather's attention honestly, with schooling well accomplished and a respectful attitude. Of his own volition, the boy had begun to attend the hall and study his grandfather when the king passed his judgments. At King Virile's invitation, Charger began to be seated at his left hand during banquets and other noble gatherings. The Piebald Prince showed himself as a youth well taught, in speech, song and dance. Put forward in the games and challenges at Spring Fest, he acquitted himself well if not remarkably. He remained a lad of few words and sober dress, but he began to attract sons of lesser nobles who made little of his birth and marred face. Yet amongst the well-born sons of the dukes and the higher nobles few deigned to notice him. These, for the most part, had already given their friendship and loyalties to Canny Farseer, son of Strategy Farseer, Duke of Buck. These fair and proud young nobles called themselves amongst themselves the Canny Court. Thus a mockery was born: they called the Piebald Prince and his friends the Motley Court, as much for the unevenness of birthright amongst them as the unevenness of Charger's complexion. And among those followers was my own Redbird, loyal as ever and speaking only truth to his prince.

Now Canny Farseer at that time was a well-grown man of high spirits, a man of thirty-four years but never wed. Some say he was wild of demeanor, quick-tongued and rash in both his wagering and his rising to the wagers of his friends. All of these things are true, as was often witnessed by Redbird and his master Copper Songsmith on the many evenings when he entertained the Canny Court. Canny was not a man to turn down a challenge, and the risks he took to win were often steep ones, but it only made all, both noble youths and maidens, love and admire him all the more. The Six Dukes began to whisper amongst themselves that he was a Farseer bred and born, and many years past the age where King Virile could have named him as King-in-Waiting, and if he had done so few would have opposed it. Nor did Duke Strategy Farseer discourage such talk, and whenever such words came to young Canny's ears he would shrug his shoulders and say it was the nature of King Virile to take his time. But as the years passed he sometimes would add, twisting his own words jestingly, that soon enough it would be his own time to take. Yet Canny Farseer smiled all the while he said such things, and no one ever took it as the man reaching for a throne not rightfully his. For it was perceived that no one else had a better claim.

At the same time those who favoured the Piebald Prince began to grow in both power and prestige. For often enough the prince applied to his grandfather, King Virile, asking for this friend a grant of land, and for that friend a better share of the taxes. The members of the Motley Court began to visit Buckkeep Castle more frequently, and to stay and hunt and ride with the king alongside their prince, and have his ear at meat and to grow in influence with him. Nor did Charger limit his friends to those of the lesser nobility. He knew all the folk of the keep by name, and their children's names. A few of the better born began to perceive the goodness in him, and more than once I heard it said that despite the marring of his face the features of a Farseer spoke loud in his looks.

My own Redbird became the prince's minstrel, and not only sang to remind him and his friends of brave deeds from the past, but also began to create his own journey-man songs about the prince and his doings – mostly his hunts, but sometimes of a kind deed done for the sake of kindness.

I was often Redbird's first audience for those songs. And as I have a fair hand with the pen, I was happy to put on paper what he sang, for I wished it to ever be remembered that such clever words were the work of Redbird the Motley Minstrel and no other. For so he came to be called, and dressed accordingly in red and black and white. Over and over my son stressed to me that Charger wished him to be absolutely truthful in what he sang, with no bragging. And so he was. And I have taken that lesson from my own son, and so what I record here is truth and only truth, even when it does not paint me fair. For so I promised Redbird this account would be.

In those days, none remarked unduly that all of those of the Motley Court shared one thing with their Piebald Prince, and that was that the beast-magic was in their families and blood. Sometimes they gathered with the Farseer court at Buckkeep for the amusements the castle offered: festivals and hunts and evenings of dance and music. But just as often they hunted separately from the true court and held their own gatherings and made their own merriment. And if dogs and hunting cats, hawks and ferrets and even goats attended their gatherings, no one made much of it.

Some will say that at these private parties they held dark ceremonies and made magic with the blood and hides of beasts, and took on the shapes of animals. Some will say that in such forms, they coupled with animals and worked other foul magic. Some will say that even in those early days the Motley Court pledged to carry the Piebald Prince to power, and them with him.

Some will sing now of how Lord Canny Farseer's horse was gored by a mad bull that nearly killed the young man as well. Some will speak of ravens that perched in trees near his chambers and followed him, whether he hunted over the fields or walked in the gardens with a woman. Some will say that even in those years the Piebald Prince sent his companions in beast form against Lord Canny, to harvest his secrets and harm his person if they could. But of these charges no true minstrel sings, for they are as false as a cruel lie can be. So my own Redbird has attested to me, and so I know.

Thus matters stood in the year the Piebald Prince turned seventeen.

In that year, on a high summer day, King Virile Farseer summoned his dukes and duchesses to attend him at a great feast. He fed them well and the wine flowed more freely than the rains of winter. Then, when all were sated and mellow of mind, King Virile made a sign. A page entered, bearing with him the crown of the King-in-Waiting, the crown worn by one who trains to be the next Farseer monarch. Seventeen years had passed since last it had been seen! This the page set on the table before the king on a cushion of rich blue velvet. All stared in wonder, and Lord Canny Farseer who, unsummoned, had still come with his father, smiled to see it there, deeming it his already.

King Virile stood, stooped with his years, yet lordly still. He spoke to them all, apologizing for any follies of his youth, but hoping that he had ruled them well and justly in the past score of years. All his nobles pounded the board and agreed it was so. Then the king told them that his years had begun to weigh upon him and the time was ripe for him to assure the training of another who would follow him to the throne. He spoke of a young man grown in their midst, well taught and modest of mien. Canny Farseer did smile like the sun rising over the land. But then the king made another sign, and there entered the feasting hall the Piebald Prince. But now he walked as they had never seen him, proud in his carriage, regally clad in Buckkeep blue, the sleeves all embroidered with silver thread. To the high dais he ascended and stood before them all at the king's side. For a time all was silent as the court looked upon him. He was a well-grown young man then, tall and wide of shoulders, though the darkness that mottled his face was thick as well, and rippled if he smiled or frowned. Yet, despite this marking, he was a well-made man: if not so flawed he might have been handsome.

Then King Virile set his hand on his grandson's shoulder, and said that regardless of who this lad's father might have been, no one could deny he was the true son of Queen-in-Waiting Caution and carried as much of the Farseer blood in his veins as any legitimate son. With that, the king formally recognized the Piebald Prince as his heir, calling him King-in-Waiting Charger and asked that his nobles accept him as such and declare him ready to assume the crown of the King-in-Waiting.

A silence stood in the hall, pressing down upon us all. Then, not with joy, but with a face full of duty, the Duke of Tilth said he would abide by his king's will. Then Bearns rose to join him, and the Duchess of Farrow. The Duke of Rippon rose, and bowed silently, looking as if his mouth were full of rotten fish that he dared not spit out.

All the while, the face of the Duke of Buck grew darker with blood, till it near was black as a dead man's. When finally he rose, he leaped to his feet, saying, "Is this how you pay back the loyalty of years, my brother? To put a bastard upon the throne of the Six Duchies?"

Yet it was Canny of Buck who stood then and coming to his father's side, grasped his sleeve, and pleaded with him in words too quiet for any man to hear. The Duke of Buck, chest heaving with his angry breath, forced himself to calm. Before King Virile could answer his younger brother, the Strategy bowed head and knee to the king and begged his pardon for his hasty words. "For any man might speak awry when a hope so long cherished is dashed away. Yet I remain your most loyal subject, my king and brother. My son likewise." Then both Strategy and Canny of Buck stood and recognized the king's choice of Prince Charger to be the King-in-Waiting.

Yet the king's choice seemed in truth to make no change at all, at first, for all continued much as it had. Charger stood at his grandfather's shoulder and listened as he passed his judgments. He sat at his right now at meals, and wore the circlet of the King-in-Waiting upon his brow, but still the most influential nobles of the court paid him little heed. Still he gave most of his time to those lesser men who had befriended him before he was proclaimed the King-in-Waiting. Still Lord Canny of Buck presided over his Canny Court, and still many a lordly parent presented a daughter to him, hoping to make a match with the young noble. For though he might be only the son of the Duke of Buck, and though every one of the Six Duchies had recognized the Piebald Prince as the heir to the throne, Lord Canny remained the heir to their hearts.

Perhaps few save my Redbird perceived that a man who holds the loyalty of many small men might have near as much power as the man who holds the hearts of a few great ones. The king began to give over power to the King-in-Waiting, as was fitting, and sometimes it was the king who sat at judgment over his noble's disagreements, and sometimes it was Charger. It was then that some of the lords of the Six Duchies began to complain that Charger was prone to decide in the favour of his favourites, regardless of right or wrong. Yet some said the opposite, saying that he judged wisely, not basing his decrees on how wealthy a man was or how noble his title, but on what was right and wrong. The truth of how it was will vary with every man that speaks of it, but I will repeat what Redbird wrote into his songs. He was a fair judge, true to honesty before any friendship or favour.

The King-in-Waiting began to make more secure the loyalties of those that followed him. To each of his friends he gave a piebald mount, the get of the Spotted Stud, and when they rode forth together to hunt, they hunted with spotted hounds. So the prince made his symbol from that which men used to mock him, and some admired him for his spirit. And his minstrel, Redbird, forsook the bright garments that most of his guild wore and donned garments of red and black and white to signify who he served.

Grants of land the Piebald Prince gave as well, and special entertainments for those who followed him. Their companion beasts were welcomed to these entertainments as well, and those who were not Witted often came with

a Witted servant or companion, so soon it seemed that to have the Wit might be a path to the King-in-Waiting's favour. Not all thought well of that, and many indeed disparaged it, saying that a man's intelligence and good heart should count more than the happenstance of being born with a kind of magic. Yet the mutterings were small, and if Canny and his father were discontent, it was an unrest that few spoke about.

Now, one morning the king awoke, and all was not well. His left arm lay cold outside the bedclothes, and the side of his face drooped and he drooled from his mouth. His left eye hung half-closed, and he could not form words to tell the healer what ailed him. Now some will tell the tale that at the moment he was stricken a great black bird alighted on the parapet outside his window and there remained, both day and night. But any that tell this tale are attempting to be prophets after the event had passed. No such bird was noticed at that time, for the simple reason that the parapet was home to all manner of feathered creatures. So minstrels who sing such a song should keep company with those who prate of dragons and pecksies. The truth of the matter was that King Virile was an old man and an old man's fate had found him.

For long days the king was ill. All his court attended him and remedies from many a healer were offered and tried but, as the days passed, though he grew no worse, he grew little better. So the King-in-Waiting took up the duties of the king, and yet he dared not declare himself king, for King Virile still lived and some said he would soon recover. Canny Farseer was one of these, and he spoke softly to his noble friends, but they spoke his words louder: that it ill befitted King-in-Waiting Charger to take up the mantle of King Virile when the king had neither offered it nor died from it. Nor had the dukes convened to beg him to wear the crown. So Charger Farseer was a man caught between, neither king nor prince, and bound to be faulted whether he shirked his royal duties or claimed them.

Now, to court at this time came Lord Elfwise and his Lady Kyart, to offer to King Virile a remedy made only in the valleys of their tiny holding in Bearns. With them came their daughter, Lady Wiffen. The remedy they brought to court proved of no benefit to the king, but none faulted them for this. Many such remedies had already failed. Yet Copper Songsmith tells that they also brought with them that which was the downfall of the Piebald Prince, and that downfall's name was Lady Wiffen. And in this perhaps Copper Songsmith sings true.

Was Lady Wiffen lovely? Not as you might think. From her mother's line she had blue eyes, and from her father's hair of midnight. Copper Songsmith says of her that she walked like a swordsman, danced like a butterfly, and laughed with the music of the wind in her voice. He also says of her that she ate like a guardsman and drank as if hollow and sang many a bawdy song more lustily than well. Copper says of her that she was as unlike a well-bred lady as could be imagined. Yet this was the woman who captivated not only King-in-Waiting Charger but his cousin Lord Canny as well. All this Copper Songsmith sings, and I will record that here, but note that Redbird himself does not say such things. Of Lady Wiffen, Redbird says that I am to say only that she came to Buckkeep Castle, and that both Lord Canny and King-in-Waiting Charger found her comely and alluring.

Gifts and attentions they showered upon her, to the astonishment of her parents and her undisguised delight. A piebald mare, a ring with three emeralds, a music box, a Jamaillian tapestry, chimes from Bingtown, perfumes from Candalay . . . each man's gift was more expensive than his rival's previous one. Two minstrels sent to sing outside her chamber window by moonlight came to blows in their masters' names, and were both well doused with the lady's wash-water. For a time, such antics amused both courts at Buckkeep, and no one disparaged the lady for being unable to decide between two such determined suitors. She might arise to ride with one, dine with the other, and dance that evening with the first one again. To Lord Canny, on his name day, she gifted a silver cup. When it was King-in-Waiting Charger's birthday, she presented him with a hip-knife with a buck's head on the hilt. Some sing that she was just a simple country girl come to court, with no idea how to deal with her illustrious admirers. Others say that her father urged her to smile on Lord Canny, while her mother matched her with the Piebald Prince.

Of these things, Redbird said this: it may have been the girl and her charms, but it seemed most likely to him that she was no more than a target for their rivalry and a cause to make their long contention loud and bloody. The competition that had festered between them since the Piebald Prince was born finally had a place where it could be clearly won or lost, with no fears of anyone saying shame upon them or muttering of traitors to the crown of the Six Duchies. If the Lady Wiffen had clearly declared for one or the other, perhaps their infatuation would have burned out within a fortnight. But as it was, what neither could possess became bitter dispute between them, and their quiet war finally gained a public face.

Redbird has said that opinions may have truth in them but that truth must be free of opinions. So, for him, I shall say now not what men speculated, but what happened. Lady Wiffen declared no favourite. As first the weeks passed and then the months, the courts' amusement turned to irritation and then open hostility. The Canny Court muttered that Charger had first stolen Lord Canny's rightful throne and now he would steal his true love. The Motley

Court rejoined that Lady Wiffen had not given her hand to anyone and that the rightful king was as free to court her as any man. The quarrel grew from pointed jests to harsh words, and yet never openly between the two rivals but always amongst the men that followed them.

Then blood was shed outside the Great Hall in a drawing of weapons based on what one man had said of the other's lord. It was Lord Ulder, of Blackearth in Buck, whose bright blood spattered the snow, and it was Lord Elkwin, holder of the tiny fief of Tower Rock in Farrow, a follower of the Piebald Prince, who shed it. The battle was swift and fairly fought, and perhaps it might have been ignored save that Ulder's wound went to foulness and pus. He died within the week, and there were mutterings of filth on Elkwin's blade, deliberately treated to cause a festering wound. On the night following Ulder of Blackearth's death, someone went to the stables. Fully a dozen piebald steeds were slain before the uproar of the other horses and dogs put the varlet to flight. Some said it was Ulder's younger brother Curl who struck such a cowardly blow, yet as no minstrel witnessed it, no minstrel should sing of it as true, and so I tell it here as Redbird himself would.

Whoever did it stabbed more deeply than he knew, for the heartstrings of a dozen of the King-in-Waiting's men were fastened to those beasts. Bonded as those Witted were to the horses, it was to them as if their beloved wives had been slaughtered in their sleep. The deaths struck them all, some with wild mourning and some with silent grief and some with outright madness, so that all was uproar within Buckkeep, and many wild vows of vengeance made. Most wounded of all seemed to be Lord Elkwin of Tower Rock, he who had slain Lord Ulder in honourable challenge. He knelt by his slain horse and tore his hair and his beard until the blood ran, and clawed his own face and screamed like a woman in childbirth.

Finally a healer was called, with both herbs and leeches to drain the madness from him. For many a day and many a night, Lord Elkwin lay in his bed in his darkened chamber and spoke no word to any man, not even when his own prince called upon him to beg him to return to his rightful senses.

It must be told here that although Charger's favourite spotted mount was slain, the Piebald Prince was not unmanned by it. He grieved, as any horseman would, and for his Witted fellows he was full of sympathy and solicitation. But if the coward who slew horses in their stalls had hoped to wound the prince that way, he failed. For his horse was not his Wit-beast, as had been long supposed. The beast that shared Prince Charger's heart and mind was a matter he kept very private, and even among his Witted followers few were trusted with the knowledge of which creature shared its life with the King-in-Waiting.

So Charger, although filled with anger and grief for his friends, kept a calm voice, even though all around him members of the Motley Court called for bloodshed. Despite the King-in-Waiting's promise that the culprit would be found and punished, some among them complained loudly that no punishment could be sufficient for such a cowardly crime.

Even so, perhaps calm heads could have prevailed, save that on the following day the king himself stiffened in his bed, thrashed and then died. The healer attending him swore that at the moment of his passing a black bird rose cawing from the parapet right outside his window, just as if the bird rejoiced in the death of the king. On so little a thing as this tale were the rumours of foul deeds and darkest betrayal based. Some in their ignorance said that the black bird had stolen the king's life essence and flown off with it. Others said it was the Wit-beast of one of the Motley Court, and that it flew off to spread the joyous tidings of a death that would bring their prince to the throne. Some said it was the king himself, turned to a black bird and condemned to live as that creature by his bastard grandson's magic. Many another wild or foolish tale was based on the healer's words about a black bird flying and cawing, and all as if that were not the most natural thing in the world for a bird to do. All of these tales were fuel to the simmering feud within the court.

So it was that although both Canny and Charger cut their hair in mourning and their respective courts followed their example and the king was honoured in the proper way, few spoke of his passing in sorrow and respect. No. All the talk was of whether the dukes would recognize the Piebald Prince as their rightful king or declare for Lord Canny; or if the Six Duchies would split and civil war bloody the land. Too quickly was good King Virile forgotten. To this day, few recognize how cleverly he had kept peace in his land.

Now, it must be recalled that it was the younger lords and ladies of the land who had so openly avowed loyalty to one or the other of the rivals. While younger hearts might sing aloud, older heads rule, as the saying goes, and so it was when the time came for the dukes to confirm King-in-Waiting Charger as the full king. Each in turn rose, and not a single one missed the chance to remind all that the Six Duchies had enemies on every border who would not hesitate to strike boldly if they did not stand together as one. As each duke or duchess spoke, so did he or she declare afterward for the Piebald Prince.

Last of all to stand was Strategy Farseer, Duke of Buck. His wife, the duchess, sat behind him, white to the lips, and his son sat behind him, and the eyes of Canny Farseer were so black that it seemed no life was in them at all. When Strategy spoke, he said he spoke the words not only of himself, but also of his son Canny who would reign as Duke of Buck after him. The wish of him and of his line was that the Six Duchies would not be divided into quarreling states, but would remain as one and strong. For none in his family, he said, loved anything more truly than their homeland. The welfare of all the people of the land, he said, was a more important concern than the ambition of any one man, and so he would bow his knee to Charger as his rightful king, since his brother had chosen the young man to succeed him. Then, to the surprise of all, his son rose and knelt beside his father, bowing his head to his rival.

King Charger, King-in-Waiting no longer, received that homage, going first so white that the color upon his face was like black mold on a white cheese, and then so red that the vein hammered in his temple. For with this act, not only Duke Strategy but also his son Canny won the acclaim of all the court, for it was perceived as a noble sacrifice of honourable men. So it was that by conceding the throne to his rival, Canny and his father won the hearts of many a man who had not thought so well of them before.

Some say it was also in that moment that Canny won the heart of Lady Wiffen. That is a chancy thing for any minstrel to sing, of the moment when a lady's heart joins itself to a lord's, so Redbird cautioned me to say only that so it seemed to be, for at the feasting of the new king she chose to sit beside the heir to the duchy of Buck even though she had been offered a place of honour at Charger's left hand. It was a strange celebration, for the man honoured had eyes only for the lady who seemed to have dismissed him, and many who sat at his table were still hollow-eyed with grief over the loss of their Wit-beasts, and spoke little and ate even less. Surely it was not an auspicious omen of a hearty reign to follow, and so it proved.

Now King Virile had died when spring was venturing toward the land, and by Springfest King Charger wore the crown of the Six Duchies upon his Witted brow. Yet as the days lengthened, the new king's reign did not prosper, but shrivelled. The rains continued chill and heavy past the time when the soil should have been warming. Those who planted lost their first sowing to rot, and the coastal storms slowed trade to a crawl, with many a cargo delayed or spoiled. Some minstrels will sing that such dreary weather foretold all that followed, but in truth, as Redbird bade me tell it, it was only weather, which cares nothing for the affairs of men.

In the sodden spring, a lone flower seemed to bloom and that was Lady Wiffen's opening heart. Lord Canny's courtship of her had prospered, and so sweet a couple they made that minstrels made song of the fondness that gentled her and stirred Lord Canny to acts of greatness on her behalf. In her name, he slew the bear that had taken more than a dozen cattle from a Buck farmer's herd. Many a feast he held in her honour, and when she presided over his table she was decked as royally as any queen in the jewels and furs and silks he bestowed upon her.

It was announced that they would wed as soon as her kinfolk could make the journey to Buckkeep to witness the nuptials. For Lord Canny himself went to King Charger and asked of him that they be allowed to say their vows before the Witness Stones of Buck and dance their wedding dance in the Great Hall. King Charger could hardly refuse this favour without looking both mean and spiteful, and so he said it might be so, but any could see that it clove his heart to do so. As fate would have it, no sooner was the joining announced than the weather turned kind, and spring seemed to rush over the land as if to make up for the lost days.

So it was that King Charger presided over the wedding feast of the woman he had hoped to claim. He sat Lord Canny upon his right hand, and Lady Wiffen upon his left, and his mouth smiled but his eyes were empty. After the couple had danced their first dance as wedded partners, then did Lord Canny, smiling all the while, offer his wife's hand to his king, that he might lead her in a dance upon the floor. What Charger said to her while they trod their measure no true minstrel heard and hence no true minstrel can say. Some with black tongues say that he threatened the vengeance of the Witted upon her family and home if she did not yield herself to his wishes, and some say that he whispered to her with his father's wily tongue that could spell any maid, and some say that he but spoke from his own broken heart, words of disappointed love and dashed hopes that would have wrung any maiden's heart. No man can know what was truly said as they spun and bowed, and so no true-tongued songster will sing of it. But whatever words passed between them, all remarked that it was a chastened Lady Wiffen that the king returned to her lord's hand, and that afterward she did not seem so merry of heart, nor so light of foot. Often and often that evening her eyes turned from Canny to Charger, and some say they saw her regret her choice as the lovelorn king sat brooding alone at his high table.

However that may be, it was too late to change it, then or now.

So off the couple went to their marriage bed, with many a lusty jest thrown after them. After they had departed, the rest of the court continued to dance and eat and drink to their happiness and to many children for them. The king, too, remained in his high seat, cheerful as a corpse, and many of those who came to join him at his high table as the evening progressed were likewise grim, for they were among those who had lost their Wit-beasts in the stable slayings. Some false minstrels will sing that that was the first time Lord Elkwin of Tower Rock had been seen clothed and on his feet since his horse was slain. But it was not so. Redbird had seen him, walking in the garden on his lady's arm, grave of mien but correctly garbed and clear of eye, every morning for nearly six days before the wedding feast. That is the truth of it and so it should be sung. Yet it is true that this was the first feast he had attended since his Wit-beast had been slain, and that he dressed and moved still as a man in the madness of mourning. So were many soberly garbed, despite the gay occasion, and some drank in a manner that was more to drown sense and sorrow than to celebrate a wedding. It seemed, some say, that a darkness began to seethe at the end of the hall where the Motley Court gathered, and that what came next was planned at the king's own high table, but as no true minstrel witnessed it, no true minstrel will sing that as so.

However it might have been, before two nights had passed, before the wedding guests had departed the court for their own homes, before Lord Canny had borne his bride off to his high hall in Buck Duchy, murder was done in Buckkeep Castle. The little daughter of Lord Curl of Blackearth, brother of the slain Ulder, was found in the stable. She was not yet seven years old, and had no reason to be in the stables at night, yet there she was found in the morning. Her throat had been slashed and she lay in the very stall where Lord Elkwin of Tower Rock's Wit-steed had died. Some minstrels will say that this alone is proof that he did it, but any fool with or without a song in his mouth can as easily see that it could be proof that he did not, for what sane man would leave such a clear signature to his guilt if he wished to commit such a heinous crime?

This, indeed, is what King Charger said to his court when his nobles convened to hear the charges that Lord Curl of Blackearth brought against Lord Elkwin of Tower Rock. That was a proceeding that brought satisfaction to no man, for again and again those who sought to speak were shouted down. The Motley Court on one side of the room accused Lord Curl with both word and glare of the slaying of the Wit-steeds, and the Canny Court shouted back that the slaying of a hundred horses could not be seen as good cause for the murder of a child. And from the rear of the crowded room rose the voice of a man far more vicious than brave, for he shouted that the dukes were fools to expect justice from the son of a Chalcedean beast-wizard. Then even the eyes of the king, who until them had seemed most in control of himself, went narrow with fury and some minstrels sing that his nostrils flared like an infuriated stallion as he flung his head back at that insult.

But others sing more truly, as Redbird did, that he was visibly incensed and yet clenched his lips and let no intemperate words escape them. The ugliness of the insult spread through the room like congealing blood and for an instant a silence fell. Then the shouts arose again, and the words that were flung were angry and wild.

No order could be brought upon them, not even though King Charger called in his own guard and ordered them to see that no noble spoke out of turn. Finally he commanded his guard to clear the room and announced that in three days they would reconvene in the hope that justice and common sense could prevail. Yet the Canny Court muttered that he did not put Lord Elkwin in a dungeon with a guard upon it, but only sent him back to his own guest quarters in the castle, and that the men the king put upon his door were ordered to protect him from attack but not to confine him to those rooms. They muttered, too, that the king had already made up his mind, and that he put the life of a spotted horse above that of a tender, dancing daughter of his realm.

Lord Canny of Buck might have been trying to calm the waters when he stayed up late with his closest followers, with Lord Curl of Blackearth in their midst, and added his voice to his wild mourning. But perhaps he was not.

The angry muttering grew to a roar, and no peace was added to it when the rumour was uttered that while Canny was drinking with his men, the king was seen walking by moonlight in the garden, and that he was not alone, but that Lady Wiffen of Buck walked with him, her hand in his.

This rumour burned through Buckkeep like a summer fire, and Lord Canny of Buck confronted the king with it as he descended the stair the next morning for his breakfast, clutching his wife by the wrist. Her face was white, her eyes red with weeping and her hair was wild upon her shoulders. Before all, Canny accused the king of attempting to cuckold him, and his marriage not a week old. Before all the court, they quarrelled, not as king and lord, but as cousins and rivals, with many a wrathful word and a reminder of old injuries flung between then.

All the while Lord Canny clutched his wife's wrist so tightly that her flesh stood out in bulges between his fingers and her hand went first red and then nearly black. When the king rebuked him for this, Lord Canny replied that she was his wife now, to do with as he wished. Before the king, his face gone black and white, could reply to this, Lady Wiffen spoke. Having stood pale-faced and quiet, suddenly she turned and raked her nails down the side of her husband's face, shrieking that to be shamed so publicly by him when she had done no wrong was bad enough, but she would not stand silent while he declared her no more than chattel and a possession. When her husband let go her wrist to clap a hand to his bleeding face, she sprang away from him and up the stairs, to take refuge behind the king and Charger spread his arms wide so she could shelter behind him and declared her to be under his protection.

Now the king's guard had arrived. In a roar like a bear Charger ordered them to remove Lord Canny and his men from the stair. This they did, and while blood was shed, no grievous wounds were dealt; Copper Songsmith was there, at the foot of the stair not far from the Canny nobles, while Redbird was at the top, behind his king and Lady Wiffen, and they both saw all of this and heard every word, so do I swear that every word I write is true. As Lord Canny went, bare swords prodding him along, he vowed vengeance, saying that his wife's mind had been turned by the Wit-magic and that King Charger had bespelled her. King Charger roared back that Lord Canny spoke of things he could never comprehend, any more than he could comprehend the pain and horror that his cowardly minion Lord

Curl of Blackearth had dealt when he slew the piebald
horses and thus brought his own grief upon himself.

All there gathered heard King Charger's rash words
of accusation, and it seemed to many – even to Redbird
Truthsinger – that the king had said he saw justice in Curl's
little daughter dying to pay for the lives of a dozen horses.
Before the afternoon had fled it seemed as if every ear in
the Six Duchies had been filled with the king's wild words.
Redbird bade me record that later the king spoke to him in
anguish, saying that the words had flown from his tongue
without thought, with never the intent of causing scandal
or implying guilt. Has any man, great or small, ever been
able to say he did not speak rash words in anger? Yet as
a minstrel sworn to truth, Redbird said I must record that
the king did indeed utter those ill words. By that afternoon, not only Charger's hasty words had spread to all of
Buckkeep Castle and town, but many a wagging tongue
added that Lady Wiffen had not just the king's protection
but also the favour of his bedchamber. This they said, even
though Charger had not been alone for a moment after the
uproar upon the stairs, and Redbird could vouch for the
truth of that.

Now all of this befell on the eve of the Solstice.

What have the false minstrels sung, sung so long and so
loud and so often, that all believe it true? They have sung
that Lord Canny of Buck, grieved at how King Charger

and his Witted lords betrayed the Six Duchies, gathered his loyal nobles and planned with them that he would face the king in single combat at noon on the Summer Solstice. They have sung, long and loud and often, that at such times a Witted one's magic is weakest. They have sung that it was done for Lord Canny's great love of the Six Duchies, and no other reason.

Yet read what I record here. Their battle was over a fickle woman and a murdered child, over a throne and a man's pride. No one could have planned such a cascade of events to have been brought to fruit on Midsummer's Day. I serve a true minstrel and what I write here is as Redbird told me, mouth to ear, and he had no reason to lie even if he had been a man given to untruth.

By the next rising of the sun, Buckkeep was as divided as a single castle could be. The Canny court and their various guards dared to go armed within the walls of the king's stronghold, and the king's men likewise. When King Charger announced to all that there would be no charges heard against Lord Elkwin, for there was as little evidence to point to him as there was to point to the man who had slain the piebald horses, he did so not from his audience chamber but from the top of the stairs that led down from his bedchamber, his guard arrayed below him. Perhaps he thought that this declaration would offer peace to both sides, that no one would be held accountable for the killing of the horses, nor for the slaying of a child done in the madness of wild grief. If so he thought, he could not have been more wrong, for each side believed itself the more deeply wronged. It might have been wiser if he had tried to offer each side satisfaction. If he had sent two nobles to their deaths, well, bloody that would have been, yet less bloody than what followed.

No sooner had King Charger finished speaking than the very woman who had sought asylum from him the day before declared herself appalled at "this denial of all justice for anyone!". While his words had been measured and his voice grave, she shrieked out her words, her eyes wild. She spoke in fury, saying that whether Witted or not, no woman thinks a beast, even her own Wit-beast, as precious as the child of her womb, and that "no number of slain horses could be put in the scales and balanced against a child murdered in the muck and straw of a stable".

Lady Wiffen spoke her angry words in the moment after the king had said his, before anyone could draw a breath. Redbird marked that the king stared at her in horror, his mouth ajar.

In the next instant, she pushed past him and stalked down the staircase, shoving aside any guards who would not make way for her, and so came to the main floor and her husband's side again. There she took her place and turned to stare up at King Charger. Lord Canny of Buck let her stand there, though he did not deign to give her a glance. A silence like death followed her words.

Then King Charger's shoulders fell, as if something had gone out of him, the very heart dragged from his body, perhaps. Perhaps he regretted those words that showed so plainly that the Witted heart feels in a way that the wholly human cannot. He did not speak again; he made no effort to defend what he had said. He turned from all, went up the steps back to his bedchamber and he closed and barred the door. His guards heard the bar thud down and accordingly they maintained their vigilance outside his door.

How was it, then, that Charger was seen to walk alone in the Women's Garden beneath the noonday sun? Some say that he turned into his Wit-beast, a rat or a weasel, and then slipped down to the garden where he resumed his own form. That is not true, of a certainty, for Redbird assured me that neither of those creatures was the Wit-beast of the king. He said also that of his own knowledge no Witted one can transform into a beast of any sort, no matter what the legends may say. As to how the king got out into the garden, Redbird said only that Buckkeep is an old castle, with secrets and ways of its own, and that a boy brought up within those walls might know more than one way out of an apparently locked room. As to why he might do so foolish a thing as go walking alone after aggravating such a man as Lord Canny of Buck, well, a man denied the woman he has set his heart on will do many a strange thing. The truth of that no minstrel needs attest to, for every man and woman knows it is so.

However it was, King Charger was walking alone when Redbird encountered him there. As to why Redbird was there, it was not an arranged meeting: when his king had retreated to the gloom of his chambers, Redbird had gone into the fragrant gardens to try to lift his own spirits. Like all minstrels of that time he enjoyed the protection of his guild and despite any unrest came and went as he pleased. His fingers were trained only to pluck strings, his voice to sing. Neither swordsman nor archer, no one had a reason to fear him.

And there he saw King Charger, head down, hands clasped behind his back, treading the winding paths through the thyme beds toward the old cherry trees. It seemed to Redbird that the king was so sunk in sorrow and so torn of heart that his mind almost was turned. The minstrel told me that he judged Charger to be in great danger, out in the open, unarmed, and with so many of his nobles furious with him, and yet he dared not rush off to summon the king's guard, for that would have meant leaving him alone. Redbird feared, too, that a sudden summoning of the guard to the gardens might trigger the very sort of conflict that he hoped could be avoided. So he greeted Charger quietly, asked him no questions and strolled with him in silence. The minstrel knew that no song could soothe the king's sore heart, nor bring wisdom to his confused mind. Silence and time might have helped King Charger to see more clearly. Silence and time might have shown him a way to satisfy all with justice. Silence and time might have done many things, but he was denied both of those things.

For as he walked with Redbird at his side, men began to approach the garden. Suddenly Charger lifted his head and gave it a shake, as if waking from a long dream. He seemed to come a little to his senses. "Assassins come," he said to his minstrel. "This is no place for a songster. Flee, little brother. And sing ever true." And Redbird, coward that he was, climbed one of the spreading cherry trees that grew at the edge of the garden and took refuge in its branches. Some will read this and think ill of him, and so he thought of himself, but he earnestly bade me speak exactly the truth of what he did, shameful as he thought it, so that all might know that even in this he spoke true and thus never doubt the truth of the rest of his tale. He had no weapon or knowledge of how to use one. All he had was a voice and a tongue, eyes that watched and a mind that remembered. In the end, those were all he could offer to defend his king.

And in a moment, he saw the truth of the king's words. How they had known to find him there, Redbird Truthsinger did not know, and no more do I. The killers came in ones and twos, and all bore blades, not sheathed, but carried naked and shining in the Solstice sun. Their faces, too, were naked of artifice and shining with hate, and their intent was as bare as their blades. As they closed upon him, Charger set his feet and waited grimly for them. King Charger stood there alone, his back to the tree, as the circle of men gathered around him. Now these are the names of those who came to that place. Lord Canny of Buck was there, and Lord Fenrew of Tilth, and Lord Tracker of Farrow. Young Lord Locks of Bearns, scarce old enough to raise a whisker, and Lord Scriver of Buck, third cousin to both the king and Lord Canny, and also Lord Holdfast of Rippon. Not one was a rightful duke, and some were second sons and one at least had no prospect of inheriting at all, and yet each was a scion of a ruling family of a duchy. These are the six the minstrels have named, and the truth is that, yes, they were there. But there was another as well.

"You know why we have come," Lord Canny told the king, and the king, unarmed and surrounded, laughed aloud with despair.

Now many another minstrel will recount a long speech that was made then, or say how Charger hissed like a snake or snarled like a wolf. Often and often was it told, even in those days, how the king drew his blade and slew young Lord Lock, and how then Lord Canny fought single-handed against him, and that the king changed his shape, from wolf to bear to giant serpent, to flame-tongued dragon to giant poisonous toad. Oh, aye, many a valiant song has been sung of that encounter. But the truth was that the king was empty-handed as he stepped away from the tree, and his enemies moved to ring him. Yet he ignored them all except his cousin but walked toward him saying, "You have the heart of the woman I love, and the hands of my nobles. You have my throne in all but name, and that is why you have come. To take from me my crown." Those are the words Charger said, just as Redbird Truthsinger recited them to me. He drew breath to say something else but what that might have been, none can say.

For Lord Curl of Blackearth was also there, and he stepped forward and without a sound or word of challenge he wrapped his arm about the king's throat from behind, choking him, then drove his short sword into King Charger's back and twisted the blade in the wound.

Young Lord Lock it was who cried out in horror at such dastardliness and leaped forward to tear the coward from his victim. Lord Curl, in the redness of his battle fury, snatched his sword from the king's back and with a swing cut the boy's throat from side to side so that he fell choking on his own blood. Then all, even the miscreant himself, stood back in horror from what he had done.

Lord Canny cried out to them all, "Blades down! Be still and think! What are we to say happened here?"

Above him in the tree, Redbird muffled his mouth with his sleeve. Terror raced his heart and grief closed his throat and cowardice left him powerless to move, but a raven in the branch above him croaked hoarsely. The king had fallen upon his face in the dirt, yet he was only sorely wounded and not to the death. King Charger stirred then, and rolled onto his side and spoke, almost with triumph, "Traitors one, traitors all, and all will swing for it." His eyes locked with Lord Canny's as he spoke his foolish words. All knew what his words did not say: that both crown and woman would be his when Canny had hanged for treason.

Those were the words that sealed his fate, for then it was that they all closed on him. There was no grand challenge and duel, no king assuming the shapes of beasts as he battled Lord Canny. They did not defeat him, and then hang him for his magic. No. There was only a frenzy of swords plunging into an unarmed man on his belly on the earth, and before it was over, not a blade remained clean and honourable.

Only one man saw what had happened. Only one man owned the truth of that moment, and he was a minstrel clinging to the trunk of a cherry tree above them, sick with the slaughter and betrayal, unmanned by his faintheartedness.

Do false minstrels sing of how Lord Canny and his cohorts cut King Charger's body into four pieces and burned it over water to keep his soul from finding his flesh again? They lie. The reason they hewed it to pieces, swords rising and falling like butchers' cleavers, was that they wished no man to see the many cruel cuts that had pierced him, and not a few in his back. The blood from their flying blades spattered up even to the lowest branches of the cherry tree, and over them all flew a raven, cawing and cawing in his distress.

Nor did they burn his flesh. At least, not while Redbird dizzily watched did they do so. Instead, Lord Canny demanded that each man take a piece of the hewn body, wrapped in his cloak, and bear it away until he could decide how they would speak of all that had happened. And when King Charger's body had been gathered, it was Canny himself who took away in his cloak the head and the circlet that still adorned it. Young Lord Lock of Bearns they left beneath that tree. It was Lord Curl who drew the king's hip-knife from its sheath and left it standing in the boy's back, as if such a short blade could have cut his throat so deeply that it near severed his neck as Curl's blade had done.

Now the tale returns to Redbird who bade me note clearly that he considered himself an unredeemable coward but a truthful one. Sick of soul and quaking with terror, he felt he could neither loosen his grip on the trees branches nor otherwise move. He stayed in the tree for all that day and through the night to the next day. Only the raven did he have for company, and the bird came and sat on the branch near him and watched him with one eye, as if to say that they alone could witness the truth of what had been done. Yet Redbird the minstrel felt he had been seized by silence. A kitchen maid came in the early morning with a gathering basket on her arm, and when she saw the body of young Lord Lock, she fled screaming. Still Redbird did not stir.

Even when men came to examine the body and shout over the king's knife in his back, and then to bear away the body of young Lord Lock, Redbird did not call out to them or come down. Even when he heard them exclaim at how low a death the boy had suffered, stabbed in the back by the king with his buck's-head knife and left in the dirt like dead vermin, Redbird was still. All that time, folk came and went under the tree, talking and gossiping of what they knew not, weaving a tale from blood on the earth and a small dirk in a boy's back. And never once did any of them look up to see the stricken minstrel and the raven in the tree.

Perhaps he would have stayed in the tree until he died, save that in his weariness and hunger and yes, terror, he finally swooned and fell from the branches to the blood-soaked earth below. There he was found by a cook's helper, come late to the garden to gather herbs, and she called the healers. They gathered him up and took him into the castle.

None could tell what ailed him, for the blackness of what he had seen had stilled his tongue and turned his eyes to staring. They all knew him for the king's minstrel and thought he had come to that spot to see where the evil deed had been done. Few thought well of him, tainted as he was now by Charger's friendship. But they bathed him, and fed him, and cared for him tenderly as is the rightful duty of a healer to any injured man. And so I will speak no ill of them.

After a day had passed, word was sent to his mother, to me, to come to take charge of my son, a man turned to a child again. And when I arrived there, I found Redbird as they had told me, staring of eye and still of tongue. And outside the window by his bed a raven sat in a tree and watched us. So the healer Nance remarked to me, saying the raven had followed them as they carried him from the garden to this bed, and as she is known as a woman who speaks true, so shall it be recorded as truth here.

I took my son back to my rooms in the keep. Alone, I urged him to walk and I took him up the stairs, a step at a time. No one aided me, but no one hindered me either. A draught I mixed for him, one long known to my family, and he plunged into sleep. A night and a full day and half a night more passed before he opened his eyes, but when he did, his soul was in his body again. And in the dark of that night, as I sat by his bed in a room lit by a single candle, his first words to me were that I must fetch the best pen and ink and vellum to write on. And when I had done so he first told me the full tale of all that had happened. Sitting in that circle of yellow light, I wrote it down as he spoke it, each word fresh and new in the telling, to be sure no drop of truth was lost from it.

Since no one had seen Redbird in the garden, none of the traitors who had slain their king knew there was a witness to their deed. Redbird lay in my room, as ill as if his body had been beaten from the shock to his heart and mind. The news I brought back to him each day grieved us both, for Buckkeep, and then all the Six Duchies, seemed to go mad. The king was missing, and the foul tale spread that he had killed young Lock and then fled his evil deed. With no man on the throne to keep order or speak of peace or measured justice, hatred flared and spread like a summer fire.

Much changed in the next ten days. I kept to my routine as far as I could, but said little of Redbird recovering in my room. The door to my chamber was always bolted. My meals with the other servants supplied me with all I needed of gossip and rumour, and all of it was frightening. I scarcely dared look out the window onto the courtyard below for fear of what I might see. All the piebald horses in Buckkeep and every spotted hound in the stables were put to the sword. Those who dared denounce such deeds were declared Witted, partaking of the king's evil magic. Many a noble of the Motley Court was beaten or simply vanished.

Any that could flee did. To be Witted had become a sign of an evil and beastly nature, low and deceiving.

By the end of the month, common men and women had been hanged for the offence of being Witted. That was when the custom of quartering the bodies and burning the parts over water began, for all sorts of tales had spread of how the Witted could change into beasts, or hide their souls in their Witted partner's body and return later to reclaim their own dead flesh. Now this was a tale never heard before, and I judged that I knew well why such an idea was being planted. To be Witted was spoken of as a taint, and children with one Witted parent were just as endangered as those who had formerly claimed the Wit proudly in their professions as animal-healers and shepherds and grooms. All, not just the truly Witted, lived in terror of being accused of beast-magic. Many – nobles as well as merchants and tradesmen – fled Buckkeep and the entire duchy of Buck, leaving behind their homes, their fortunes and even their names. It was a blood-letting such as Buck had never known.

The Duke of Buck, Strategy Farseer, brother to dead Virile and father to Lord Canny, tried to calm the wild seas that pounded the throne, but he was elderly and not in the best of health. He pointed out that he was the rightful heir to the crown, but he was man enough to refuse to take the throne while the king to whom he had sworn

allegiance might still be alive. The other dukes and duchesses of his realm were not so high-minded. Every evil that
had befallen the Six Duchies for the last score of years
were laid at the feet of the Piebald Prince and the Witted
ones he had raised to power. They spoke of his absence as a
blessing, and for the first time in many years even the lesser
courtiers gossiped openly that the Farseer line had been
polluted by the blood of a Chalcedean slave who was a
beast-wizard. It was time, they said, for the crown to go to
one of true and pure lineage, someone who could redeem
the Farseer line from the depths to which it had fallen.
They called for Canny to step forward and don the crown
that his father had not claimed.

They knew King Charger was dead. This perhaps my
Redbird would not sing as a truth, but I saw it in their
hard eyes. They never feared that the king would reap-
pear to claim his throne. Even then, I believe, they were
concocting the lie that would explain why no body had
been found. Their cowardly slaughter of King Charger was
being transformed by false-hearted nobles and minstrels
who cared only for the favour of the powerful and nothing
for the truth. But, to be true to Redbird, I shall write here
that the flat truth is that I have no proof that any of them
knew, save those who had been present at the murder.

So. My Piebald Prince was dead. I mourned alone for
the babe I had held at my breast, for the boy who had not

forgotten me when he no longer needed me, for the prince who had elevated my bastard son to be his truthsinger, for the man who had always smiled at first sight of me. I mourned him alone for I dared not speak of how my grief tore me. Redbird was sunk so deep in sorrow that I feared if I added my burden to his, he would drown in it and die. He was all I had left, the only one in the world who might look at me with love. And so, unbelieving, I spoke to him of better days and hope for a future that neither one of us could imagine. Without the protection of King Charger what hope had we, Witted or not? When I left the room, I did so either early or late, taking what I needed from what was left in the kitchens, no longer claiming a place at the servants' table, but striving to move around unnoticed.

All these changes at Buckkeep Castle transpired in less than thirty days, still with no proof that the king was fled or dead. And all that time, within my room, Redbird dwindled and mourned. He was too lost in his grief even to shear his hair as he should have done for his dead king. He changed his clothes only when I demanded it, and washed his face only when I set the bowl and cloth before him. He ate little, picking at the trays I brought up from the kitchen, letting the soup go cold and scummy, the warmed bread turn to stale crusts. My son shrank and soured, it seemed to me, hating himself because he was a truthsinger and not a warrior. He poisoned himself with self-disgust, and I was powerless to stop him.

Now in that time, Canny had taken Lady Wiffen back to his side and his bed. Whatever rift there had been between them seemed healed. Her hand was on the back of his wrist when they entered the feasting hall, and she rode at his side when he went out to the hunt. And when, two months after her wedding, she began to exhibit the signs of a woman with child, the Canny Court rejoiced and urged Canny Farseer ever more urgently to ascend the throne. They wanted 'an untainted Farseer' to wear the crown.

By then, the rumours had begun to circulate that King Charger was no more. There was no proof of it, and yet men nodded and smiled coldly when his name was spoken, often with a curse attached to it. Slowly the story began to leak and swirl into the minds and mouths of all the servants. Lord Canny Farseer had saved the Six Duchies. Soon would come a time when the full tale could be told.

Canny Farseer chose Harvest Fest as the time when he would take the crown. Whatever his father thought of this, he kept it to himself, while the other dukes assented easily to his claim. The Witted folk, both great and small, had been driven from Buckkeep. All of Buckkeep, both castle and town, was deemed cleansed of the Witted taint. Despite the poor spring the harvest promised abundance and this too was attributed to Canny Farseer, as if a mere man could take credit for such a thing. But folk are easily persuaded of such things. A strong and handsome young Farseer stood ready to ascend the throne, and the future queen's belly already swelled with the heir. An aura of well-being had begun to suffuse the air despite the lingering stench of blood spilled on the earth. All folk, both great and small, seemed weary of the savagery they had witnessed, and were more than ready to declare that with Canny's ascent to the throne all was now well.

Within my chambers, Redbird had fully come back to himself. He had spent many days in dark dreams or silent staring, tormenting himself for his cowardice. He had spoken only to me of what he had witnessed.

The day for Canny Farseer's crowning drew nigh, and still Redbird kept to his bed and still the raven perched outside my window. Canny had declared the court purified of beast-magic and now that his labours were finished, he was ready to be king of the cleansed kingdom. Only when I reported that announcement to him did Redbird stir. "Fetch me my harp", were his first words; and his second request was, "Find me a pen, Mother, and set out the best vellum we can buy, for I would make a song for King Canny's coronation." He spoke those words merrily, more cheery than he had been in weeks, and yet my heart sank to hear them. I feared what he intended.

Yet still I brought him the ink and the plume and the

vellum. He plucked strings softly and muttered words to himself, and then went back and tried other chords and other words. I came and went as quiet as a mouse. Isolated in my rooms, Redbird worked on his song and all the while the raven sat on the sill and kept watch over him.

The day before King Canny's coronation, the song was finished. I returned to my room to find Redbird rolling up the scroll that held his words. He sealed it with wax and pressed into the wax his sigil. Then, with a sigh, he set it down beside an identically sealed scroll on the table before him. It was then he gave me my instructions: that he wished me to copy his song in my best hand, and to write down in my own words all he had told me. "Then you must hide my tale where it will be safe from those who would seek to destroy truth, and where wise men may find it a decade or a century hence."

My heart went cold at his words. "Why must they be written down? Surely you will sing this song a thousand times."

He looked at me, sadness in his eyes, his head tilted to my words and then told, perhaps, the closest to a lie that he had ever uttered. "Perhaps I shall indeed, Mother. Perhaps I shall." Then he patted my hand. "But all the same, I shall ask you to see to the safety of these scrolls as I have asked. For I believe I shall be remembered for this song as I am for no other."

Redbird had not been invited to sing at the coronation. Doubtless many thought him dead or fled, for in all that time he had kept to my room in the keep and none had seen him. He had been the Piebald Prince's friend, and then the Witted King's minstrel, and well we both knew that all would now regard him with disdain if not hatred. It shames me to admit it now, but the truth I will tell, as he bade me. I thought he was going to seek to curry favour with the new king, that he would sing a song to honour King Canny. It saddened me to see my son so broken, but he had never been a brave child, and given what he had witnessed, I believed he had chosen the wiser path. We would bow our heads to the change in our fortunes, and somehow we would go on.

The coronation was to be held in the Great Hall, as was the custom, for everyone was welcome to witness the event. He bade me go early so that I would have a better view. Yet I did not go to see Canny claim a bloodied crown, but to hear my son sing and to hope that all went well for him. And so I chose a spot that few others would envy, for I went to the upper galleries and stood where I would have at best a view of the left corner of the throne, for from there I could clearly see the minstrel's dais where they would be called to perform to honour the new king.

Long I stood, and others came to pack in around me after the better vantage points were taken. I was hot and my head ached and my legs pained me long before the high folk of the keep entered. And when the dukes were seated on their cushioned and gilded chairs and when the lesser nobles had found their places on benches and all were settled, at last the musicians struck up a grand tune, and Lord Canny Farseer and Lady Wiffen entered. Slowly they paced to their high seats, and though I wondered at the absence of the Duke of Buck, no one near me commented on it, and so I chose to keep my silence as well.

This lordly one and that lordly one took a turn to speak, and all of it was the same: here before us was Canny of Buck, the heir to the crown and throne that his father, as King Virile's brother and next in line for the throne, had ceded to him. To hear them speak, King Charger and Queen-in-Waiting Caution had never even existed. Tears came to my eyes and doubtless those near me thought me a sentimental fool to be so patriotic during those dull speeches, but in truth grief wrenched me.

Then Canny Farseer stood and accepted the will of his dukes and agreed that he would accept the crown of the Six Duchies. Then came all five dukes walking in slow procession and bearing among them the crown on a blue cushion. And at that, a sigh of wonder and a mutter of curiosity went up, for had not that crown vanished when the 'pretender' to the throne had disappeared? And though Canny Farseer had been grave of mien up to that moment,

I swear that I saw a smile pass briefly over his face, so greatly did he enjoy the crowd's astonishment. Then he held up his hands, his arms spread wide for silence, and promised that now all would be revealed to them.

Copper Songsmith rose to come and stand before the assembled dukes and the would-be king. The years had passed unremarked between us and he had never seen fit to claim his son, even though the resemblance was such that none could have missed it. He and I had never been more to one another than a few bumps in the night. Yet he had taken Redbird as his apprentice, and somehow I had expected better of him. I was surprised at how deeply wounded I felt when he took up his instrument to strike up a fine and stirring melody and then in his lovely resonant voice, accompanied by his clever fingers on his harp all ornamented with turquoise and opal, sang as dark a string of perfectly rhymed lies as has ever been sung. The refrain was stirring and memorable: a quatrain about how the purity of his Farseer blood pounded in his veins as Canny did that which he knew he must do, and slew the beast-wizard who sought to take the Farseer throne.

It had to have been all arranged, and yet it seemed so spontaneous. As Copper Songsmith sang of how Canny had triumphed in his battle with the evil Witted enchanter, and how he had stooped to lift the disgraced crown from the dirt and wipe the stain of tainted blood from it, the dukes passed the crown from hand to hand until at last the Duke of Bearns set it up Canny Farseer's head.

And at that there rose such a roar of approval that every person in the hall who had been seated came to his feet. People stamped until the stones rang with echoes and cries of "King Canny! King Canny!" and deafened us all.

And so it was done. The crown was set on his brow and the cheers rose. His dukes retreated and returned again with a crown for Lady Wiffen and she became Queen Wiffen Farseer that night. And while all watched the royal pair, my eyes sought for my son and found him at last.

I had not marked him when he entered the Great Hall, for he was dressed all in black rather than his usual piebald attire, and a tight-fitting cowl of black scarfed his copper locks from sight. My eyes ran past him, pitying the wandering minstrel so wan and worn before I looked again and recognized my own son. Sometimes it takes seeing someone you love as a stranger to notice all the changes to them. Illness and sorrow had hollowed his cheeks and sunken his eyes so that he looked a decade older than he was. I doubt that even his own king would have known him at a glance, and surmised that all there thought him murdered or driven away with the others of the Piebald Court. So he stood, suddenly an old man, neglected in the corner, while lesser minstrels stepped forward one by one to sing of the queen's beauty or the king's bravery.

Then someone called for Copper Songsmith to sing again of how the king had slain the Witted Pretender. And so Copper stepped forth and once more sang his lies, embroidered with all the artifice of a master minstrel. Once more all heard of how the king had challenged him, vowing to break the enchantment he had put upon his wife, and how they had fought, with Charger constantly changing from one beast to another, each more terrible in form, until at last Canny slew him by hewing his great bear's head from his massive shoulders, so that the evil enchanter fell to the earth once more in the form of a man.

Silence held in the hall through this telling, though a brief cheer rose again when Copper sang once more of how the king had rescued the dishonoured Farseer crown. Quiet washed back through the Great Hall as this time Copper finished every verse, telling how the king called forth his most trusted friends to help him to do what he knew must be done to ensure the slain beast-wizard did not rise from the dead. They hewed his body and burned it over water, and thus the dreaded beast-magic was vanquished and the Lady Wiffen's mind cleared of the cloud the Witted one had put upon her.

A lone tear rolled down that lady's cheek, and she leaned her head against her husband's shoulder. Many a sympathetic sniffle I heard amongst those gathered, and I found myself wondering how much of this falsehood

Wiffen herself believed. Then my eye fell on my son, and dread rose in me. For as Copper Songsmith swung into the final refrain of his falsehoods, I marked how Redbird slowly stood taller and how his eyes began to burn.

Every coward may know one moment of courage. So it was with my Redbird. For in the deep of evening, as the queen herself pressed the prize purse into Copper's cupped hands, Redbird Truthsinger pushed his way through the crowd to the cleared space before the throne and the false king who sat upon it. Then, before all the court, he craved a boon of King Canny, that he might make gift to him of his last song before he departed the court of the Farseers for ever. King Canny raised his brows, plainly unaware of who stood so boldly before him. To this day, I think Canny believed him a wandering minstrel hoping to earn a few coins with a flattering tongue.

The end is swiftly told. Redbird set his harp before him and struck a commanding chord. For a brief time he played but notes, but they were of a power and progression that stilled tongues and drew the attention of all present. And then, louder and more clearly than ever he had sung before, he told his truth. He sang of King Charger walking in the garden alone, and how his minstrel had come to join him and how the king had bid Redbird flee. He spoke of climbing the tree and, name by name, he sang of those who had come and how they had ringed the unarmed king.

Faces paled and the king stared, while at his side his queen sat as stiff as if turned to stone. Redbird's voice was true and strong, but abruptly King Canny seemed not to wish to hear the end of the song. No sooner had he begun the verse that told how Lord Curl drove a knife into King Charger's back and himself killed young Lord Lock than King Canny cried out that the minstrel was a traitor. A dozen men, anxious to prove themselves loyal to the new king, sprang upon my Redbird.

He had never been a hearty man, and his long confinement had made him only more frail. A big man kicked him hard, driving his harp into his breast. He flew backwards, already limp. I heard his skull crack as his head struck the stones. He did not move again. I shrieked, over and over again, but my cries of anguish went unheard amongst the screams of anger and horror that rose from those around me. Then the room spun and had there been room for me to collapse, I would have. But the press of bodies held me up and though I felt as limp and paralyzed by horror as my son once had been, I had to see that which is burned still into my memory: the guards dragging Redbird's lifeless body from the Great Hall.

And then, quite suddenly, a raven glided suddenly down from the high corner of the Great Hall. He fluttered and he jibed, like a day-bird baffled by the shadowy hall and the flaring

torches. Then, as he swept low, causing people to duck, he made a final swoop and struck from King Canny's head the crown he had falsely claimed. As men shouted and ladies shrieked and all cowered away from his passage, he circled the hall three times, cawing as he did so, the queen shrieked and sought shelter behind the false king's throne. From the left and the right folk pressed and surged against me as they sought to flee the gallery. The king shouted angrily for an archer, but the raven vanished as he had come, swooping over men's heads as he flapped his way out of the Great Hall.

A panicked girl pushed me hard and as I fell to my knees she clambered over me in her panic to escape. Battered and half-trampled, I crouched, hands over my head, adding my wild sobs of sorrow to the cries of fear and anger that filled my ears. When I finally came to my senses, enough time had passed that the king and his dukes were gone, and half the gathering fled as well. I pulled myself to my feet and staggered back to my room. Alone. Alone, as ever I will be now.

And so Redbird's tale ends. It took all the courage I could muster to go to the guards and asked after the body of the last minstrel. They told me harshly that he had been judged a Witted one, and hanged and quartered and burned over water, and thus there was nothing left to claim. Some were mocking as they spoke, but one old man had the grace to be ashamed. And as he hurried me away, he told me in a hushed voice that the wandering minstrel had been dead when they took him from the hall.

So now I shall roll this scroll around the one my son made, and a second one as well, as he asked of me. One seal I have broken, for I wished to read every word of his last song, the one he was not allowed to sing to the end, to see if he had guessed that which I now know. He did not, and as a truthsinger, he would not have written that he could not verify. But I can and I will. So I will end this account as I began it, by speaking of events to which Redbird was not a party. And yet I will vouch for the truth of them with as honest a tongue as ever a minstrel had, and will put my truth alongside his, to be found a day or a decade hence.

A winter of storms followed King Canny's coronation. The hunting was bad and an ice storm such as we had never seen before broke the roofs on two grain warehouses, leaving us short of bread for the first time anyone could remember. At Buckkeep Castle, the court was less populated than it had been in previous years. The storms kept folk inside, the long days were dreary and the superstitious began to see ill omens in every broken cup or sputtering hearth-log. The queen had fainting spells and twice it was feared she was losing her child. A storm that lasted three days lashed Buckkeep Town so that the main dock was carried off on the waves and two ships sank despite believing themselves in safe harbor. Just as the weather began to warm, a disease swept through the byres and many a cow lost her unborn calf in blood and lowing. I would have blamed the poor hunting on the fools who had killed our best hounds for the crime of being spotted, and the disease on the fools who had driven away the Witted folk who once had tended Buckkeep's stables, coops and barns. Instead, many saw it as a curse put on the castle by the Witted folk, and throughout all the Six Duchies persecution of them grew only the harsher.

Yet all winters must end, even those infused with grief and injustice. Spring came, and with it kinder weather. Thaws melted the snows and the early crocus began to bloom. The queen became less pale and sickly and ate with a better appetite and her child swelled her belly. Farmers planted and as the fields began to sprout, Queen Wiffen was delivered of a boy-child, hale and hearty. His birth was celebrated far more than even the birth of a prince deserved, for all seemed to feel it marked a turning point and an end to our ill fortune. The heir secured the throne and the Farseer line. All would now be well.

And when the prince was two months old, I stood with the others to watch his name bound to him in the old Farseer tradition. Courage was his name, and his father passed him through the flames and poured the earth over his head and chest and dunked him well. All saw it as a good omen when the boy sputtered, sneezed and then laughed aloud for the first time in his life.

That laughter spread throughout the observers and as the boy was lifted high, I joined in. For as King Canny elevated the naked prince that all might behold him, I looked on proof that he was truly the rightful heir to the crown. For on the back of the child's left arm, I saw that which I had seen also on his father's arm; a small birthmark in the shape of a dark bird with outstretched wings.

And so I write here, in a clear hand, as my son Redbird would wish, the truth of the prince's lineage. Prince Courage Farseer, may he prosper and rule long, is the son of the rightful king, King Charger Farseer, son of Queen-in-Waiting Caution Farseer, daughter of King Virile and Queen Capable Farseer. And grandson of Lostler of Chalced, stablemaster and Witted one.